D0407889

BABYMOUSE AND FRIENDS*

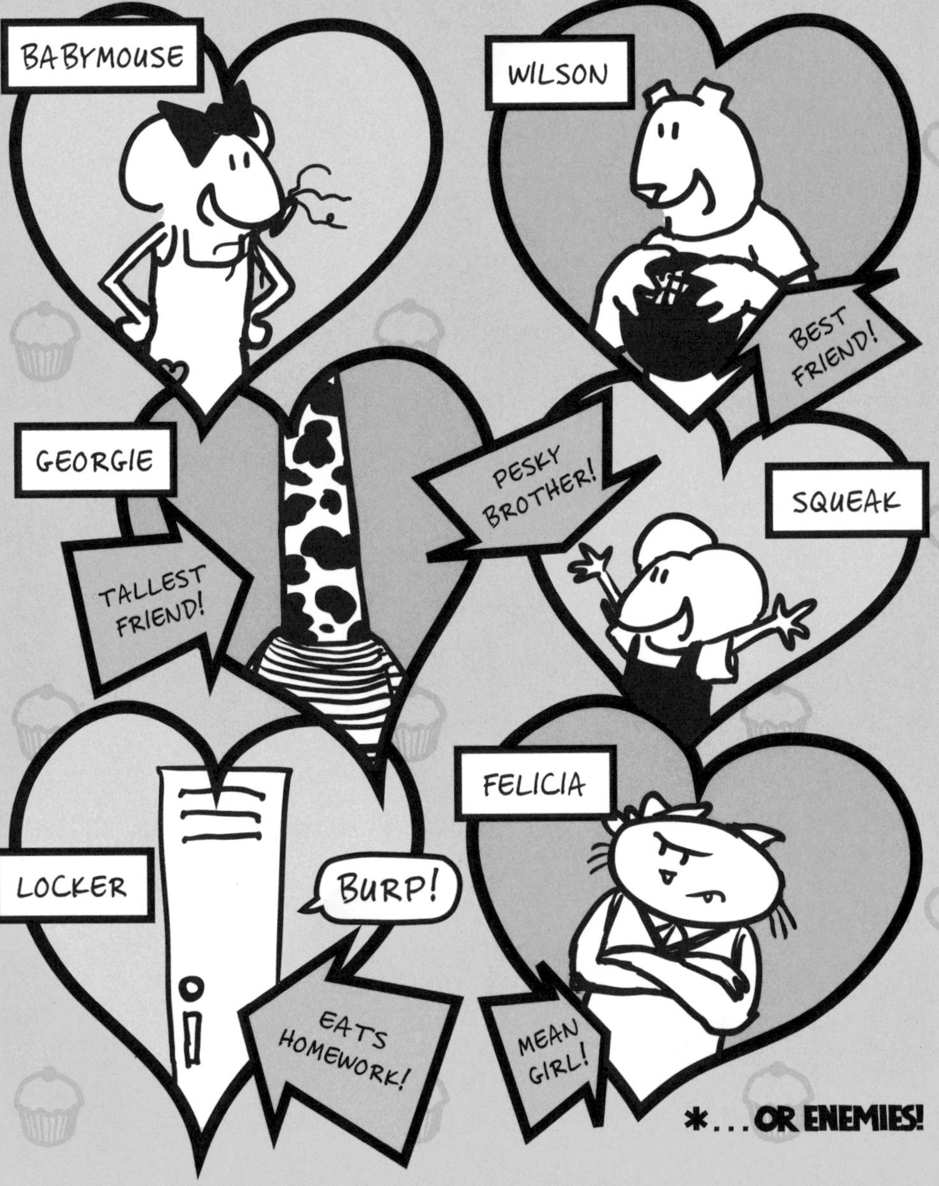
BABYMOUSE
WILSON
BEST FRIEND!
GEORGIE
TALLEST FRIEND!
PESKY BROTHER!
SQUEAK
LOCKER
BURP!
EATS HOMEWORK!
FELICIA
MEAN GIRL!

*. . . OR ENEMIES!

Be sure to read **ALL** the **BABYMOUSE** books:

#1 BABYMOUSE: Queen of the World!
#2 BABYMOUSE: Our Hero
#3 BABYMOUSE: Beach Babe
#4 BABYMOUSE: Rock Star
#5 BABYMOUSE: Heartbreaker
#6 CAMP BABYMOUSE
#7 BABYMOUSE: Skater Girl
#8 BABYMOUSE: Puppy Love
#9 BABYMOUSE: Monster Mash
#10 BABYMOUSE: The Musical
#11 BABYMOUSE: Dragonslayer
#12 BABYMOUSE: Burns Rubber
#13 BABYMOUSE: Cupcake Tycoon
#14 BABYMOUSE: Mad Scientist
#15 A Very BABYMOUSE Christmas
#16 BABYMOUSE for President
#17 Extreme BABYMOUSE
#18 Happy Birthday, BABYMOUSE

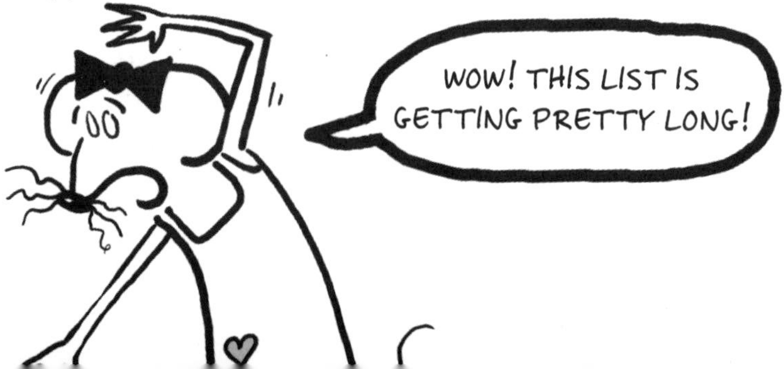
WOW! THIS LIST IS GETTING PRETTY LONG!

BABYMOUSE
Dragonslayer

BY JENNIFER L. HOLM & MATTHEW HOLM

RANDOM HOUSE 🏠 NEW YORK

HEY! I THINK THEY SHOULD PUT MATT'S NAME FIRST! HE DOES ALL THE DRAWING!

Published in the United States by Random House Children's Books, a division of Random House LLC, a Penguin Random House Company, New York.

Random House and the colophon are registered trademarks of Random House LLC.

Visit us on the Web!
randomhouse.com/kids
Babymouse.com

Educators and librarians, for a variety of teaching tools, visit us at
RHTeachersLibrarians.com

Library of Congress Cataloging-in-Publication Data
Holm, Jennifer L.
Babymouse : dragonslayer / by Jennifer L. Holm & Matthew Holm. — 1st ed.
   p. cm. — (Babymouse ; 11)
Summary: An imaginative mouse who likes to read heroic fantasy novels finds herself on the school math team as it prepares to compete for the coveted Golden Slide Rule.
ISBN 978-0-375-85712-6 (trade) — ISBN 978-0-375-95712-3 (lib. bdg.)
[1. Graphic novels. [1. Graphic novels. 2. Imagination—Fiction. 3. Mathematics—Fiction. 4. Contests—Fiction. 5. Schools—Fiction. 6. Mice—Fiction. 7. Animals—Fiction.]
I. Holm, Matthew. II. Title. III. Title: Dragonslayer.
PZ7.7.H65Baf 2009   741.5'973—dc22   2008051110

MANUFACTURED IN MALAYSIA   20 19 18 17 16 15 14 13 12 11 10 9 8 7   First Edition

33614080638199

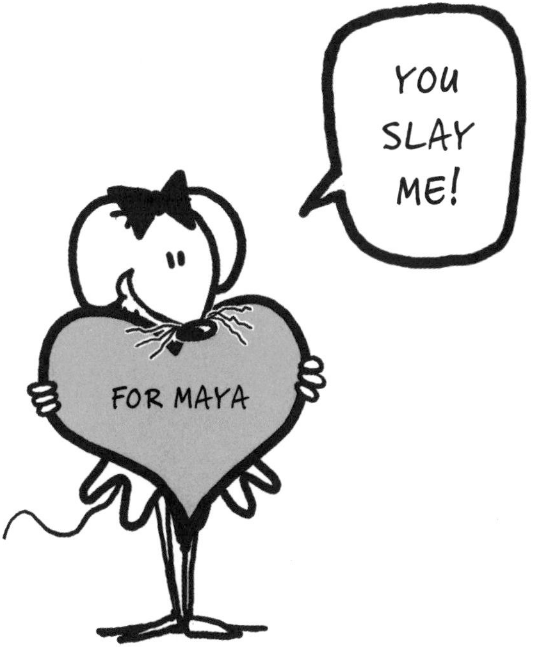
YOU SLAY ME!
FOR MAYA

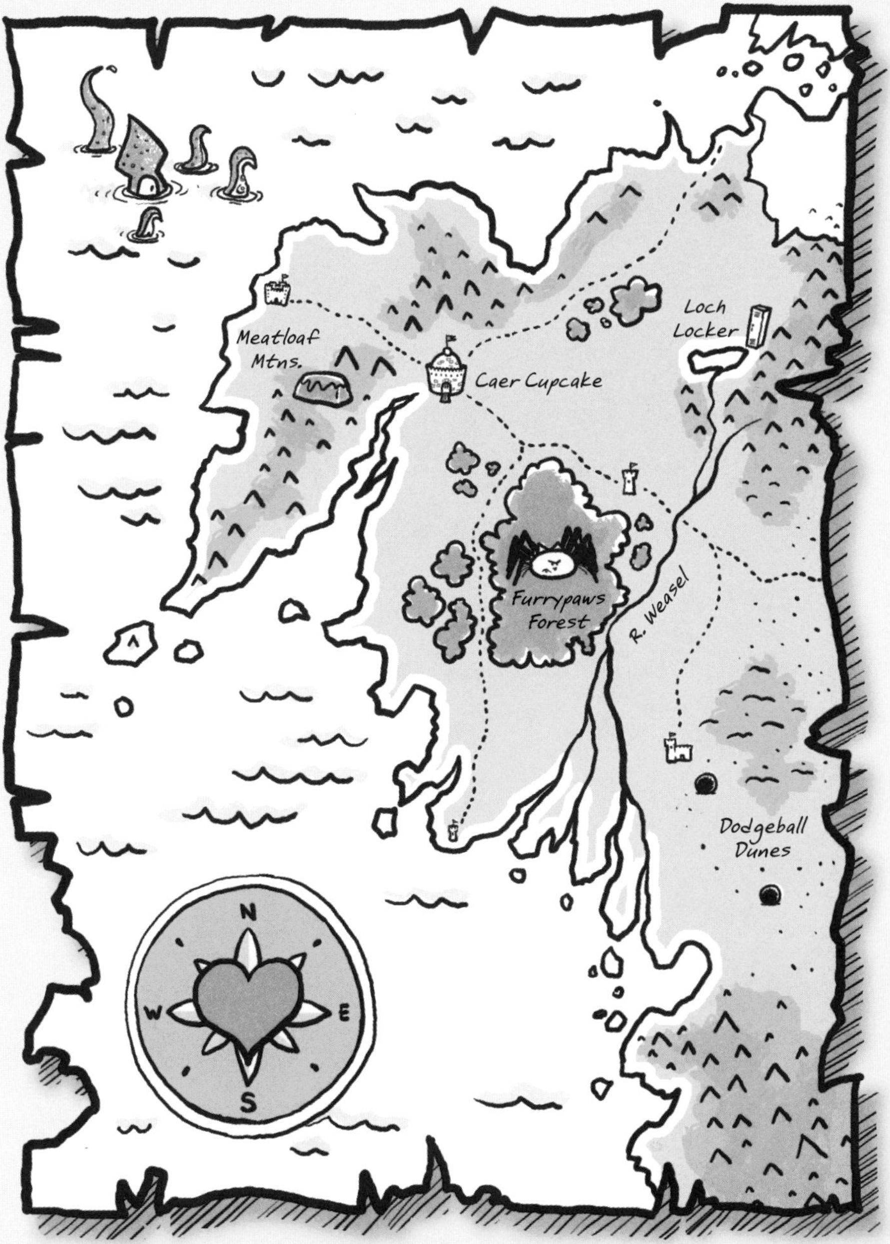
Meatloaf Mtns.
Caer Cupcake
Loch Locker
Furrypaws Forest
R. Weasel
Dodgeball Dunes
N
S
W
E

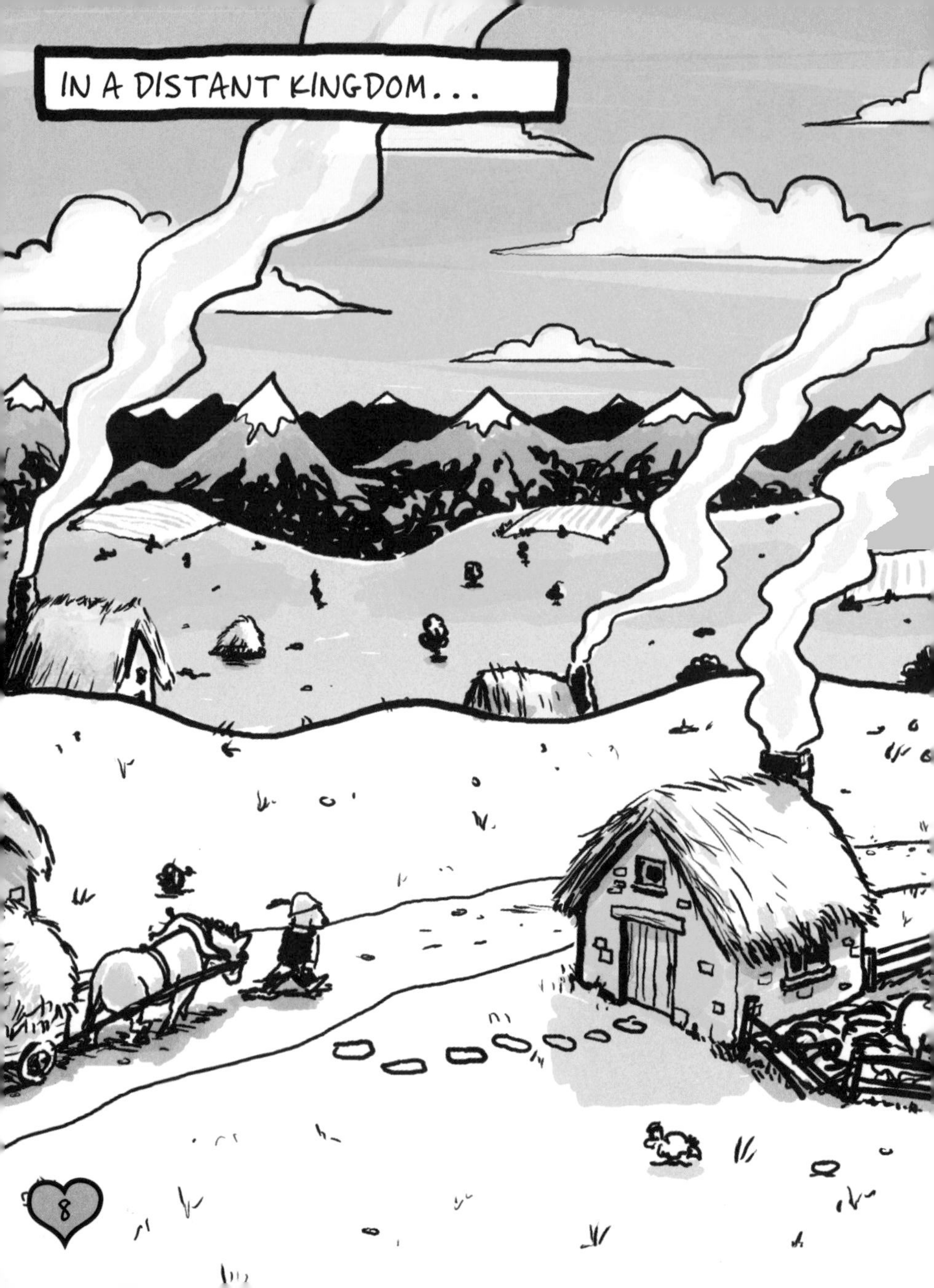
IN A DISTANT KINGDOM...

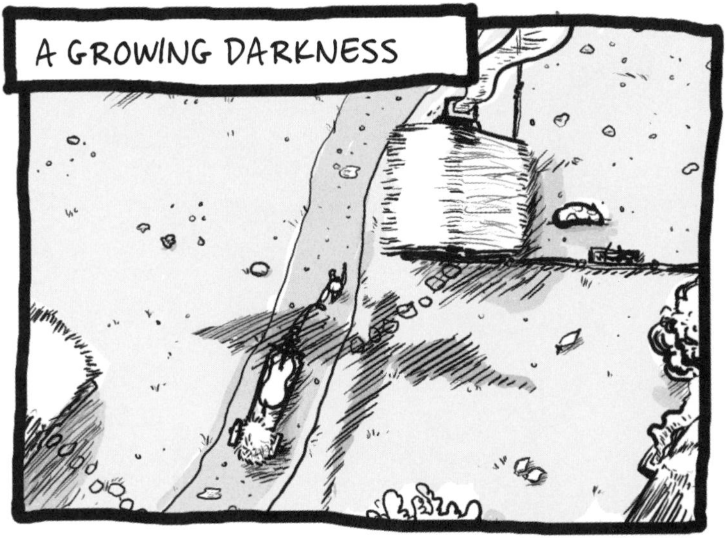
A GROWING DARKNESS

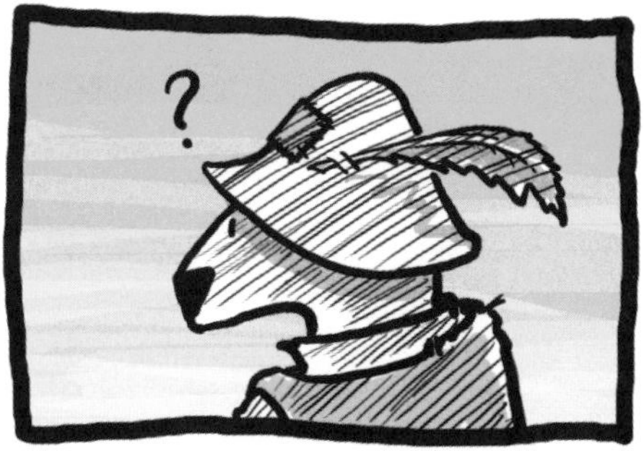
?

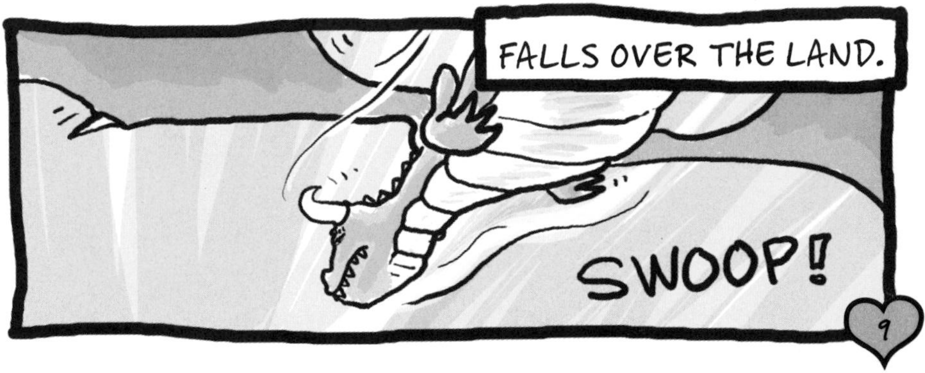
FALLS OVER THE LAND.
SWOOP!!

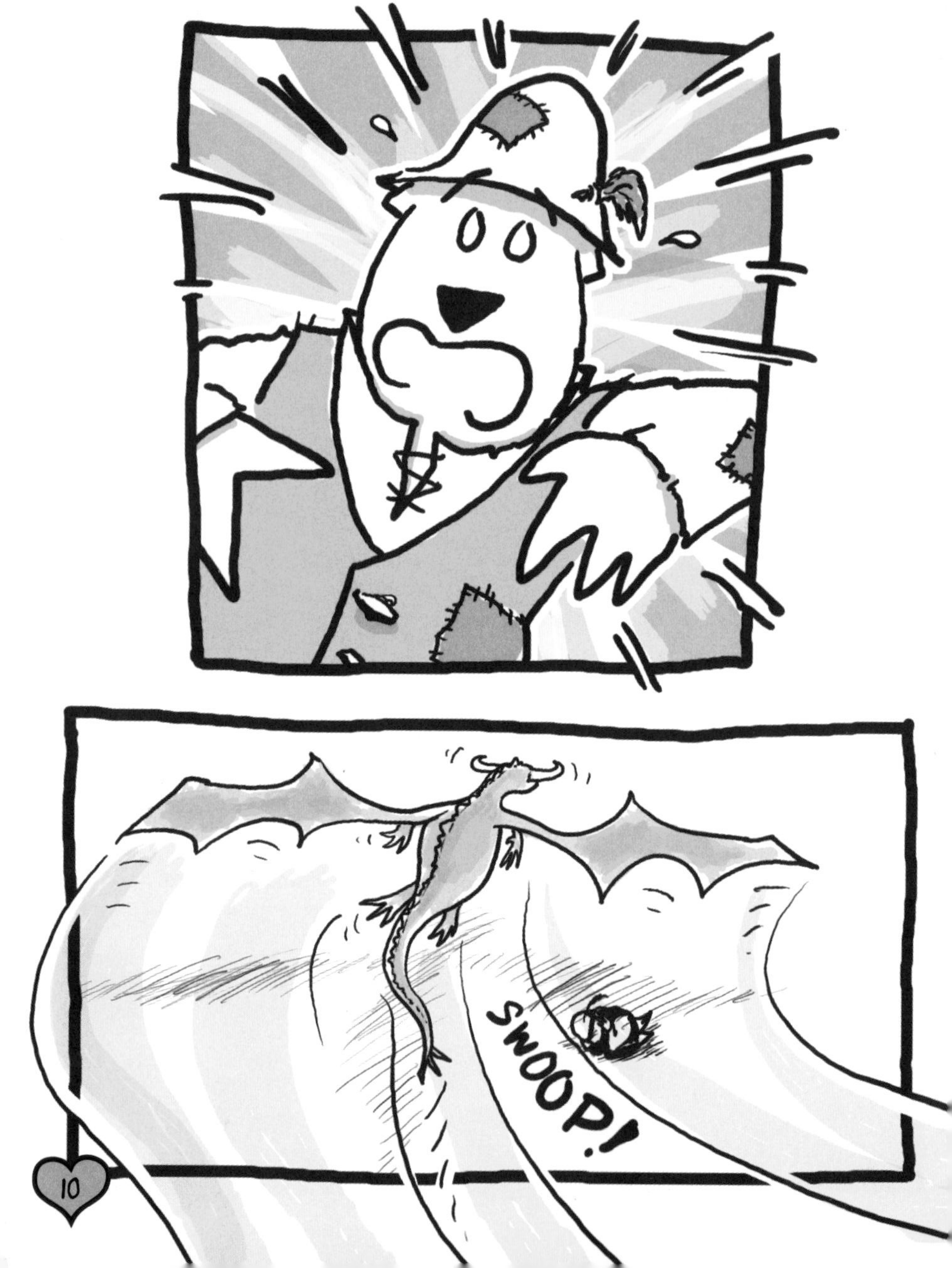
SWOOP!

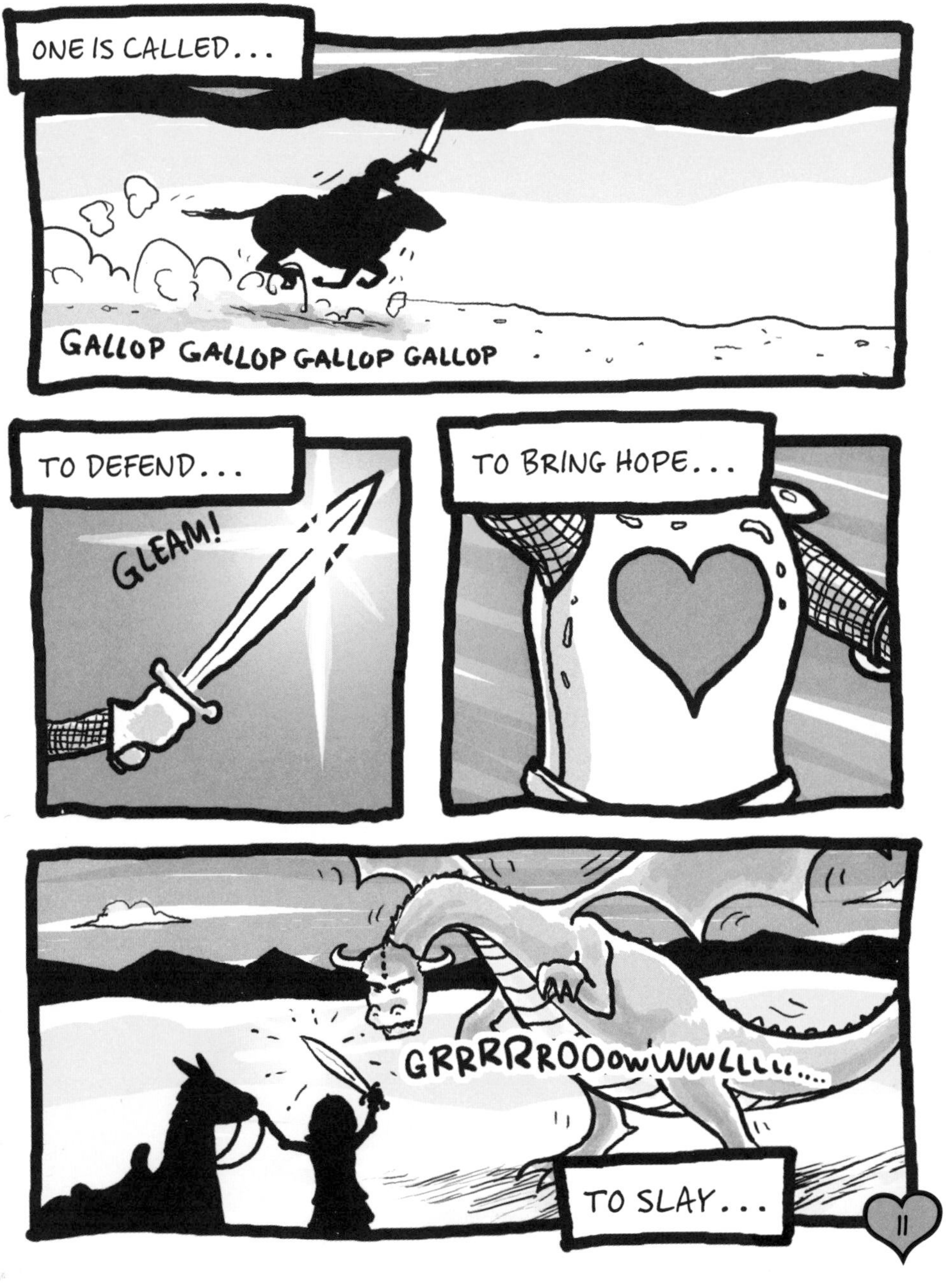
ONE IS CALLED...
GALLOP GALLOP GALLOP GALLOP
TO DEFEND...
GLEAM!
TO BRING HOPE...
GRRRRROOOowWWWLLLLL...
TO SLAY...

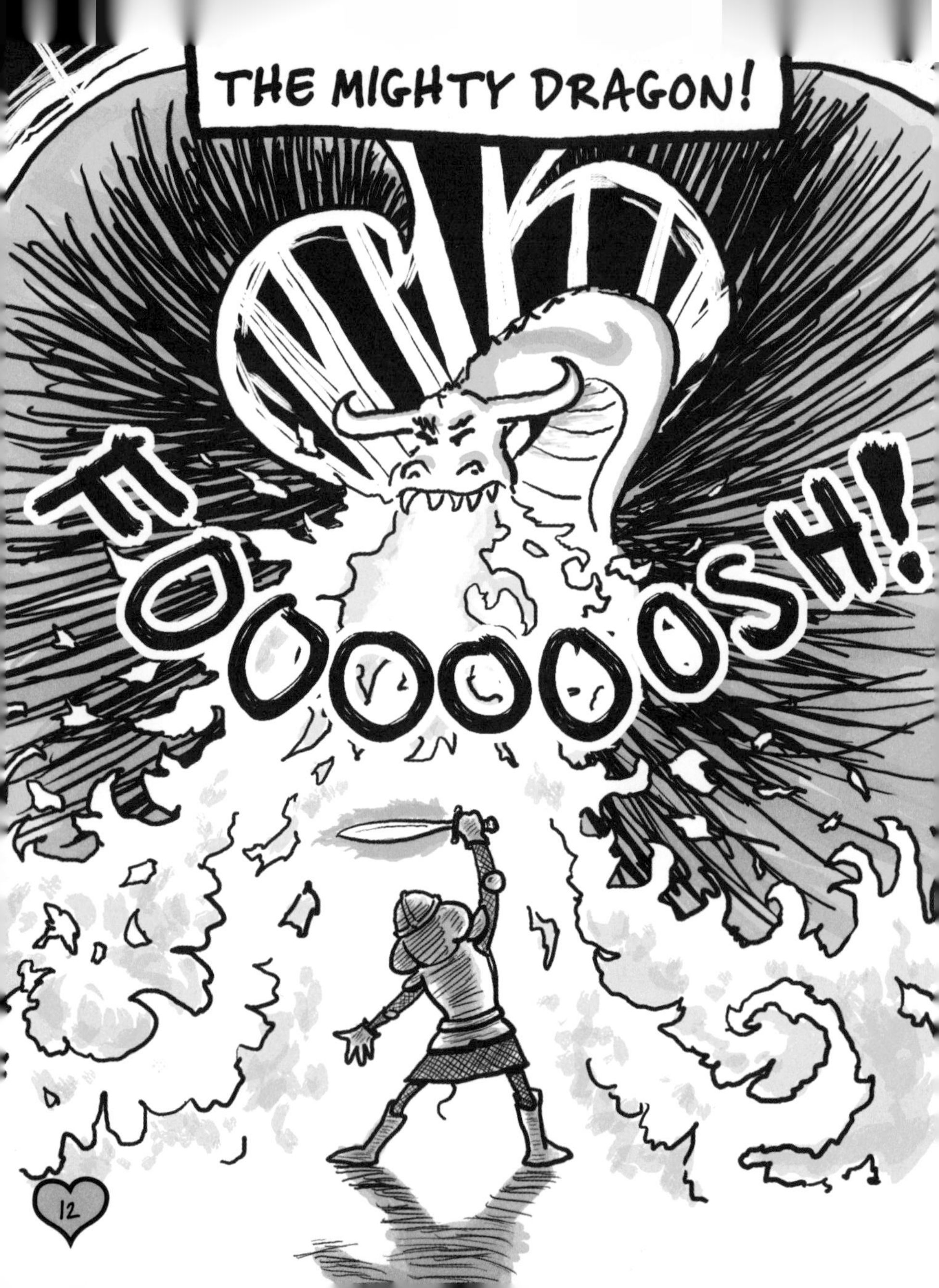
THE MIGHTY DRAGON!
FOOOOOOSH!

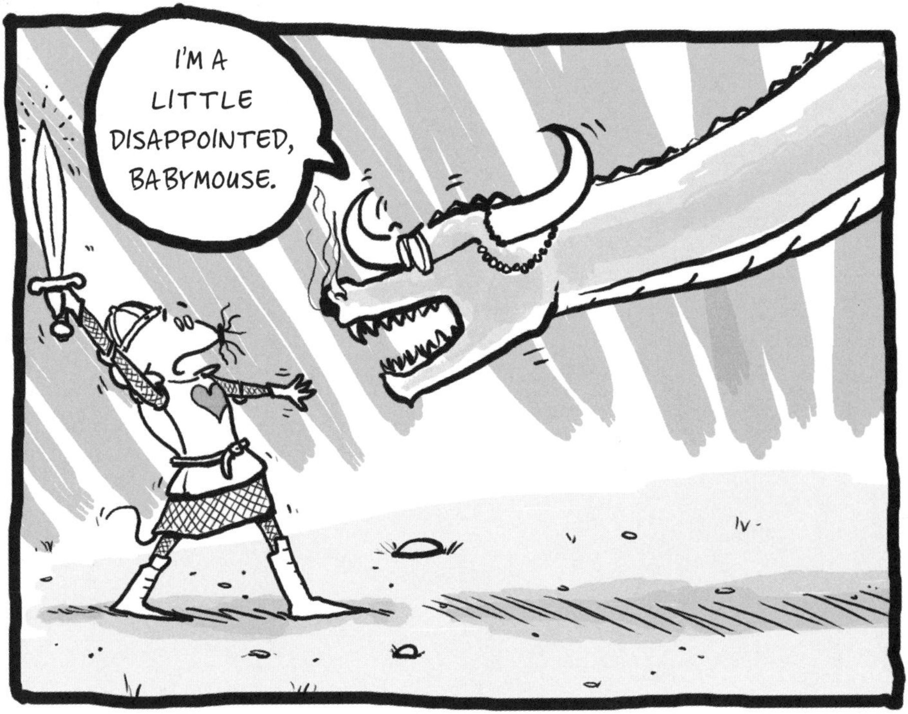
I'M A LITTLE DISAPPOINTED, BABYMOUSE.

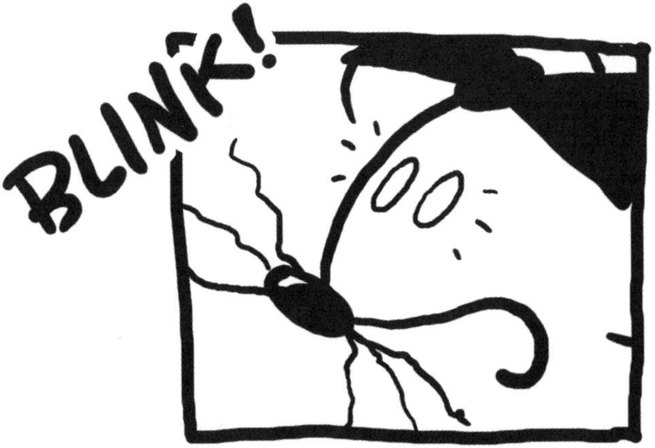
BLINK!

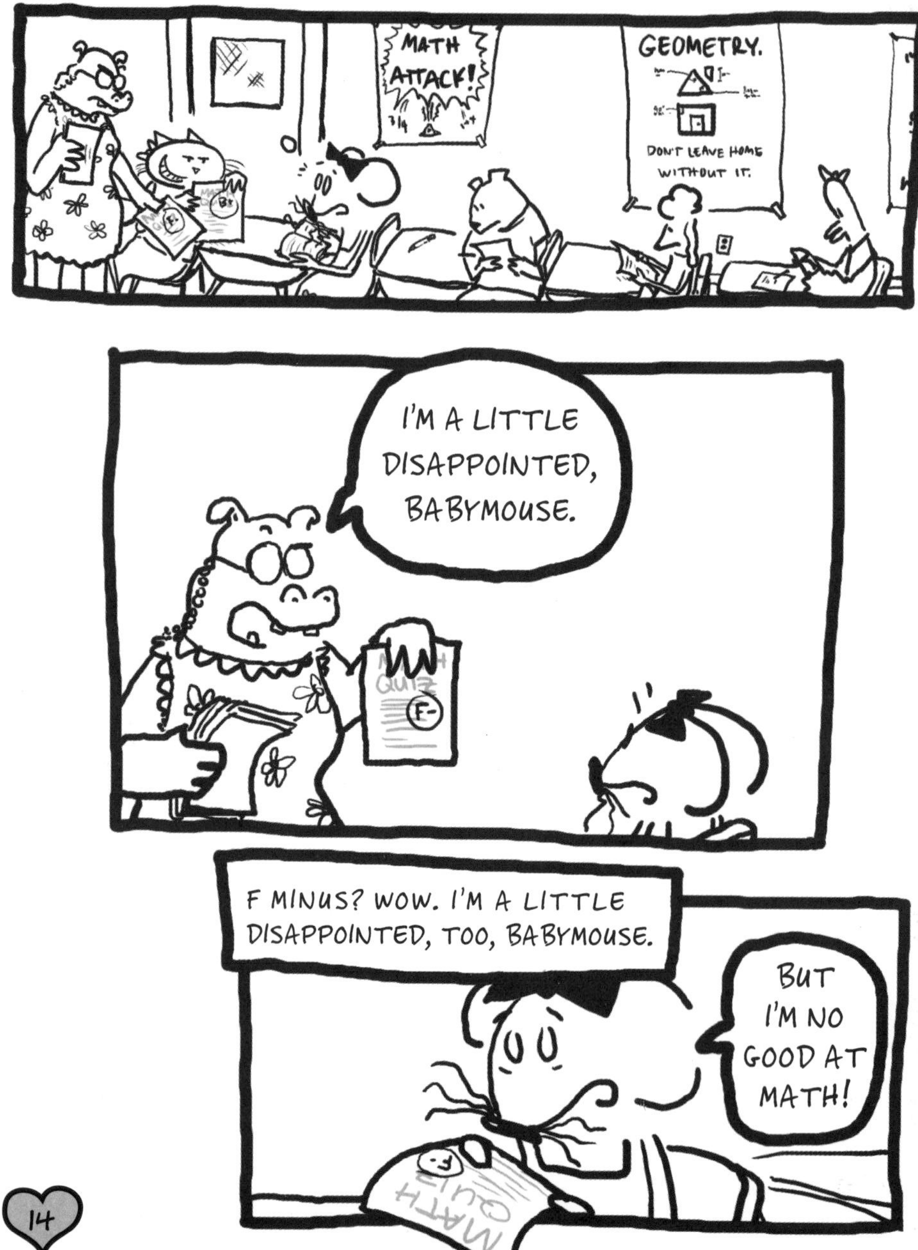
MATH ATTACK!
GEOMETRY.
DON'T LEAVE HOME WITHOUT IT.
I'M A LITTLE DISAPPOINTED, BABYMOUSE.
MATH QUIZ
F-
F MINUS? WOW. I'M A LITTLE DISAPPOINTED, TOO, BABYMOUSE.
BUT I'M NO GOOD AT MATH!
MATH QUIZ

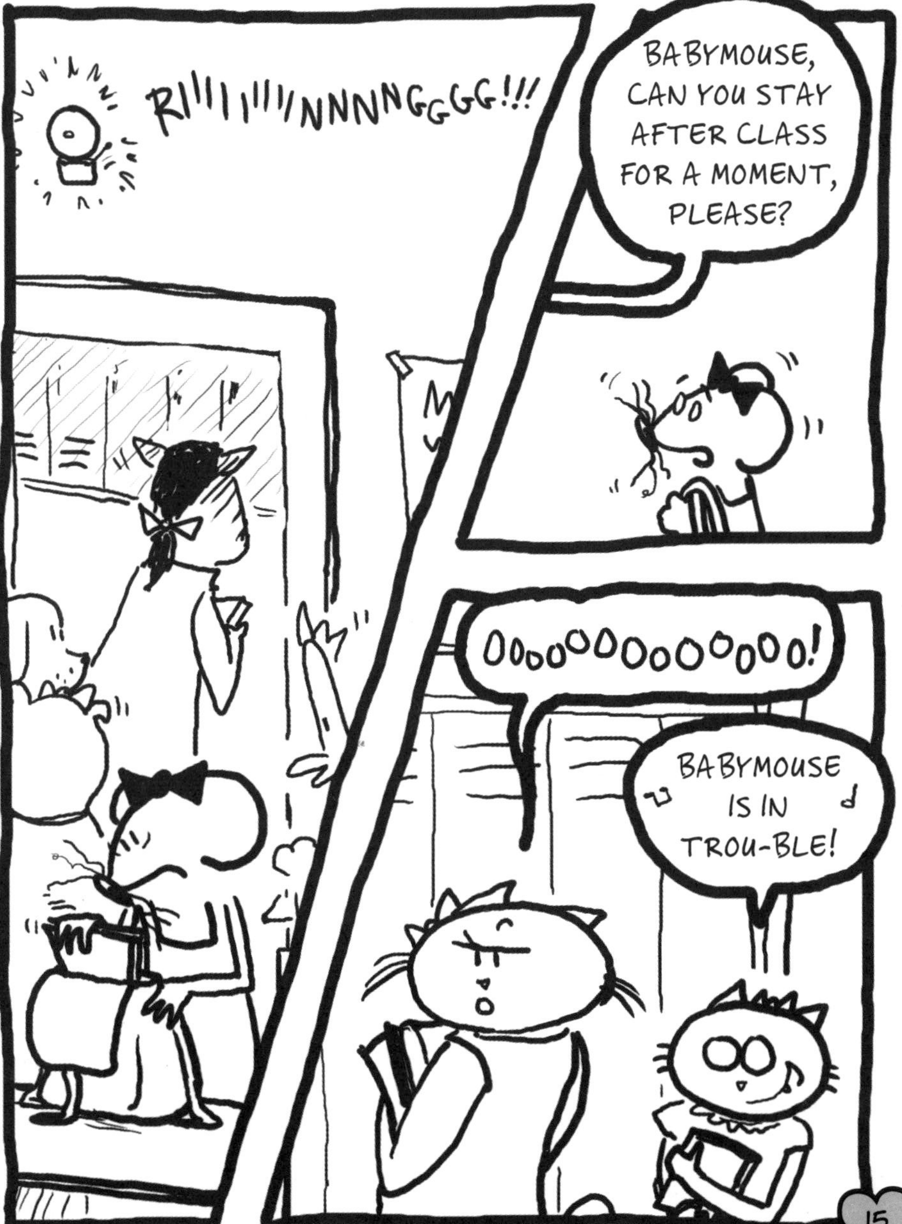
RIIIIIIIINNNNNGGGG!!!
BABYMOUSE, CAN YOU STAY AFTER CLASS FOR A MOMENT, PLEASE?
OOOOOOOOOOOOOO!
BABYMOUSE IS IN TROU-BLE!

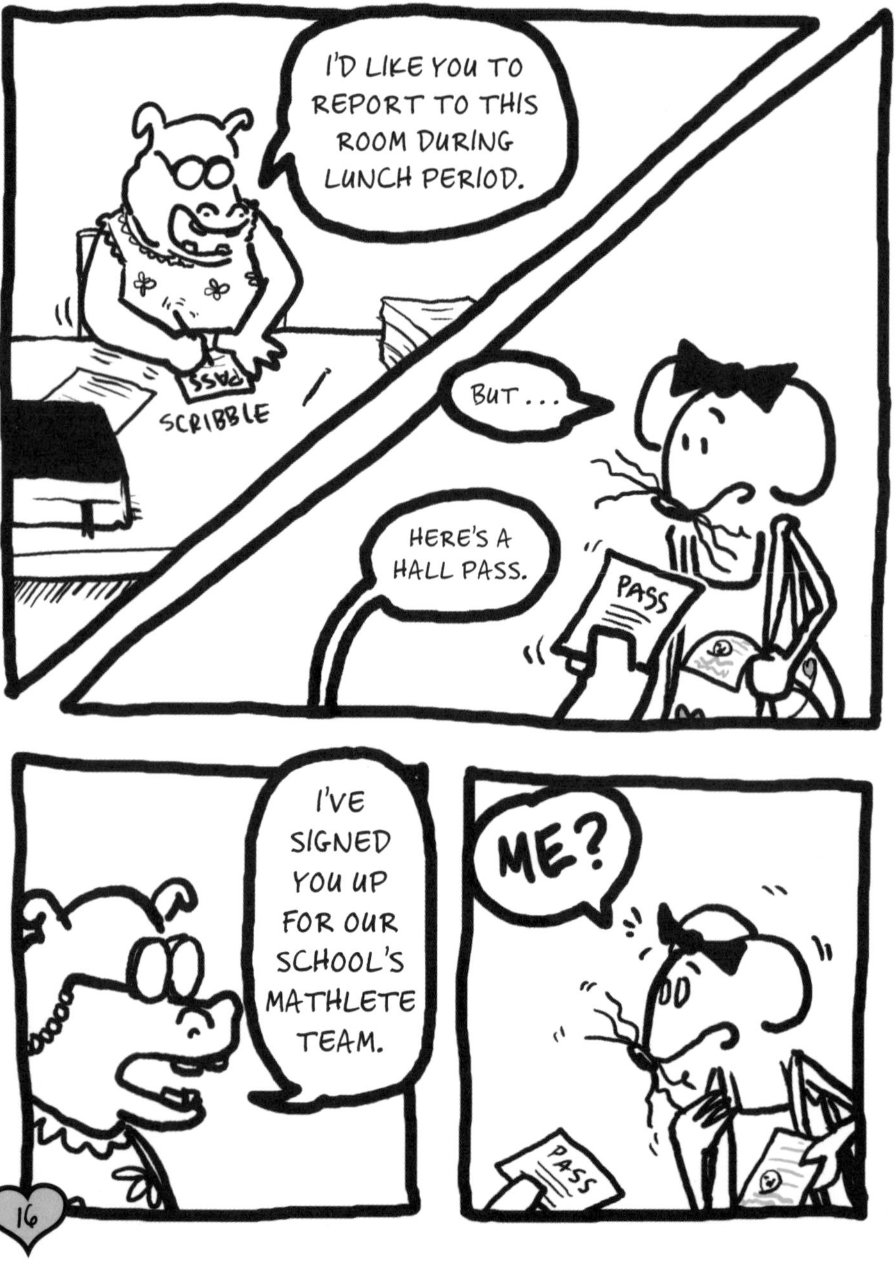
I'D LIKE YOU TO REPORT TO THIS ROOM DURING LUNCH PERIOD.
PASS
SCRIBBLE
BUT . . .
HERE'S A HALL PASS.
PASS
I'VE SIGNED YOU UP FOR OUR SCHOOL'S MATHLETE TEAM.
ME?
PASS

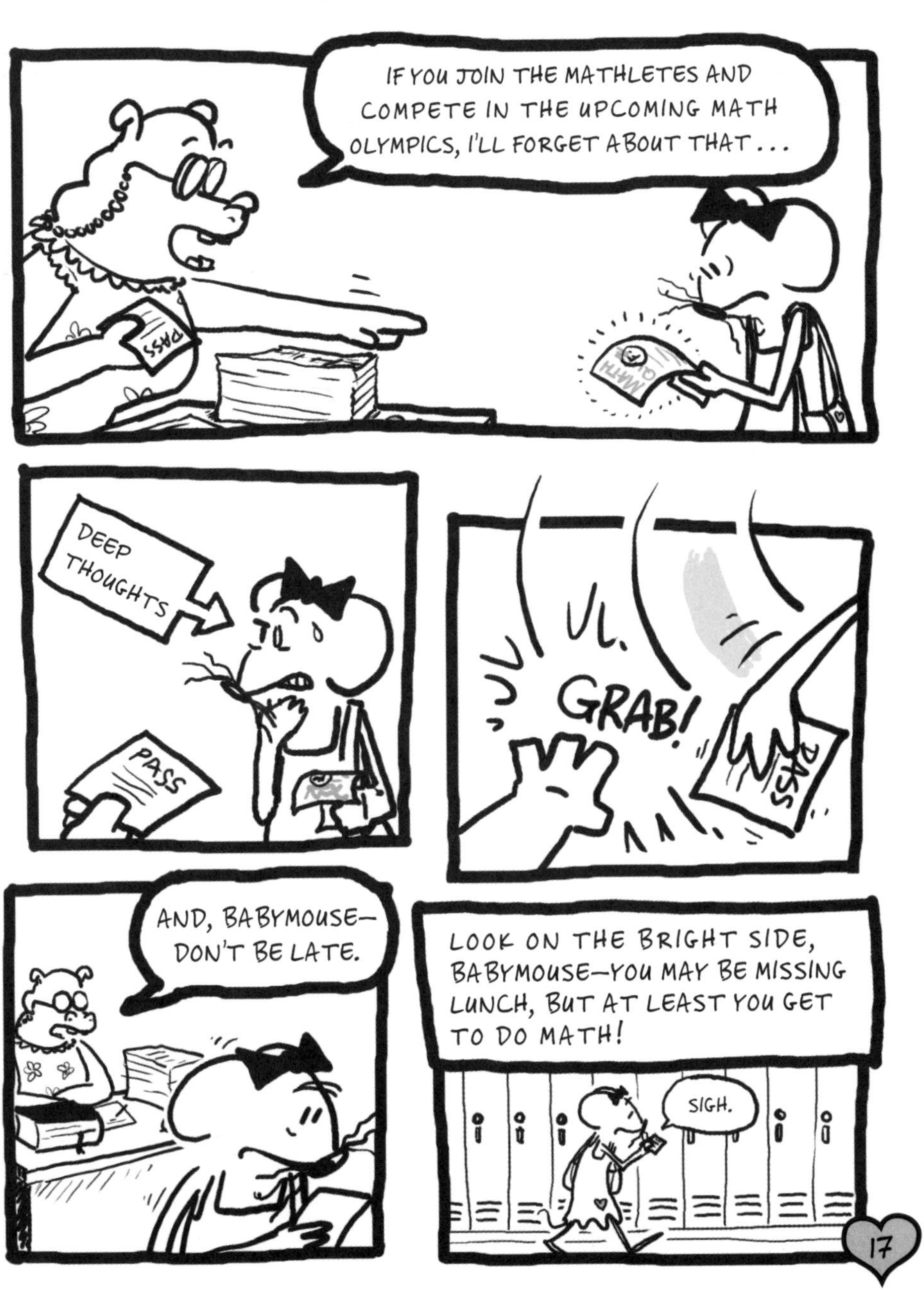

IF YOU JOIN THE MATHLETES AND COMPETE IN THE UPCOMING MATH OLYMPICS, I'LL FORGET ABOUT THAT . . .
PASS
MATH QUIZ
DEEP THOUGHTS
PASS
GRAB!
PASS
AND, BABYMOUSE— DON'T BE LATE.
LOOK ON THE BRIGHT SIDE, BABYMOUSE—YOU MAY BE MISSING LUNCH, BUT AT LEAST YOU GET TO DO MATH!
SIGH.

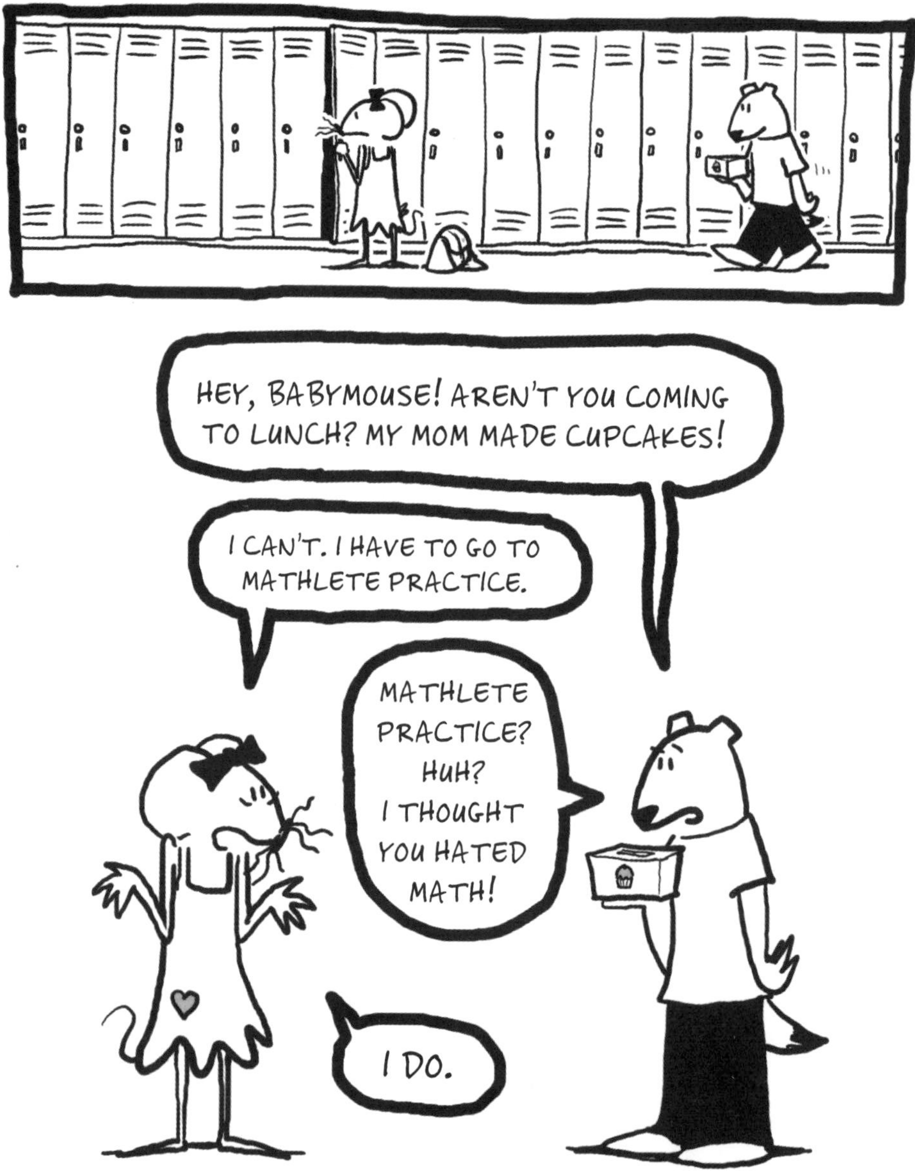
HEY, BABYMOUSE! AREN'T YOU COMING TO LUNCH? MY MOM MADE CUPCAKES!
I CAN'T. I HAVE TO GO TO MATHLETE PRACTICE.
MATHLETE PRACTICE? HUH? I THOUGHT YOU HATED MATH!
I DO.

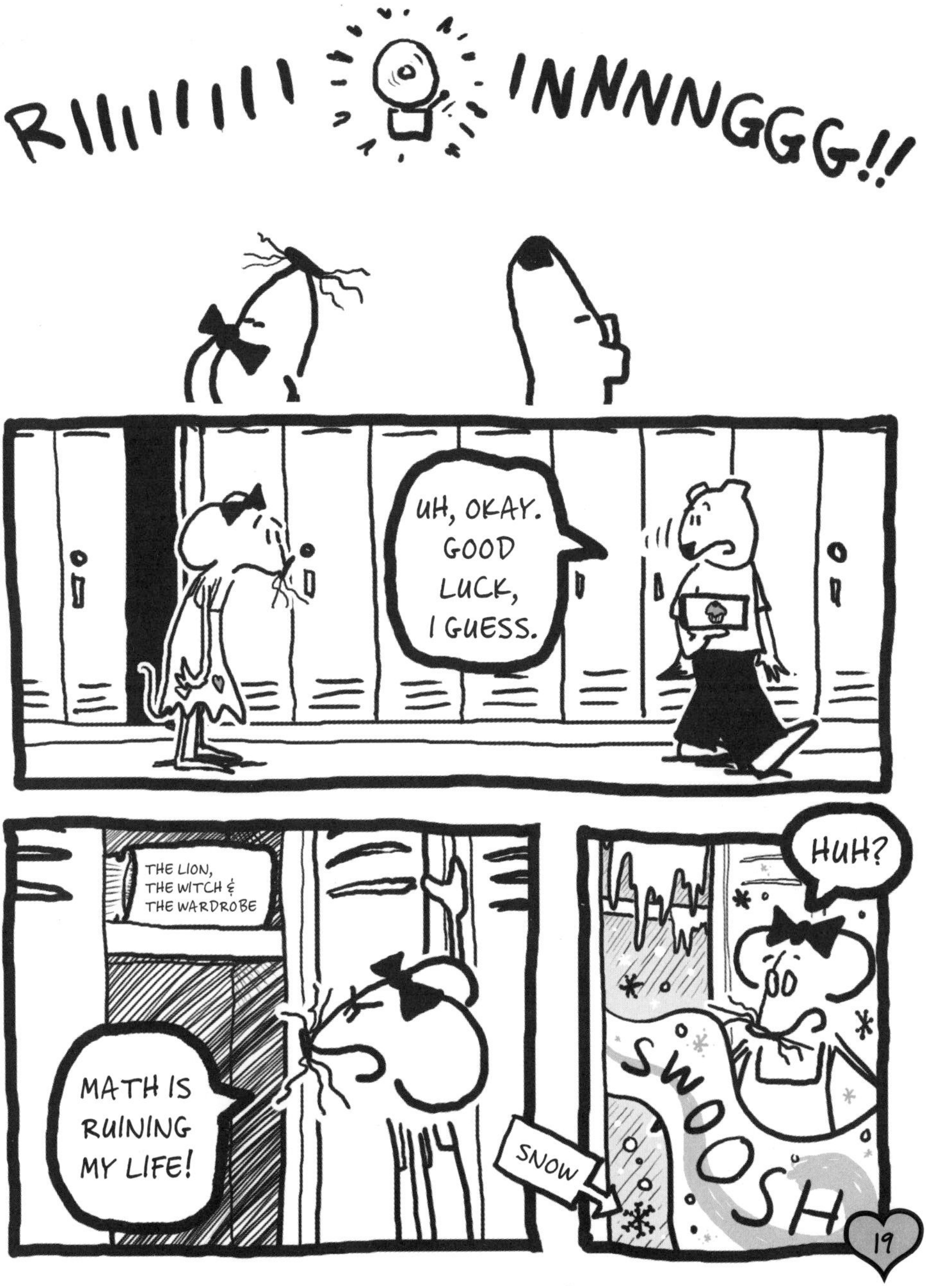
RIIIIIIIII INNNNGGG!!
UH, OKAY. GOOD LUCK, I GUESS.
THE LION, THE WITCH & THE WARDROBE
MATH IS RUINING MY LIFE!
HUH?
SNOW
SWOOSH

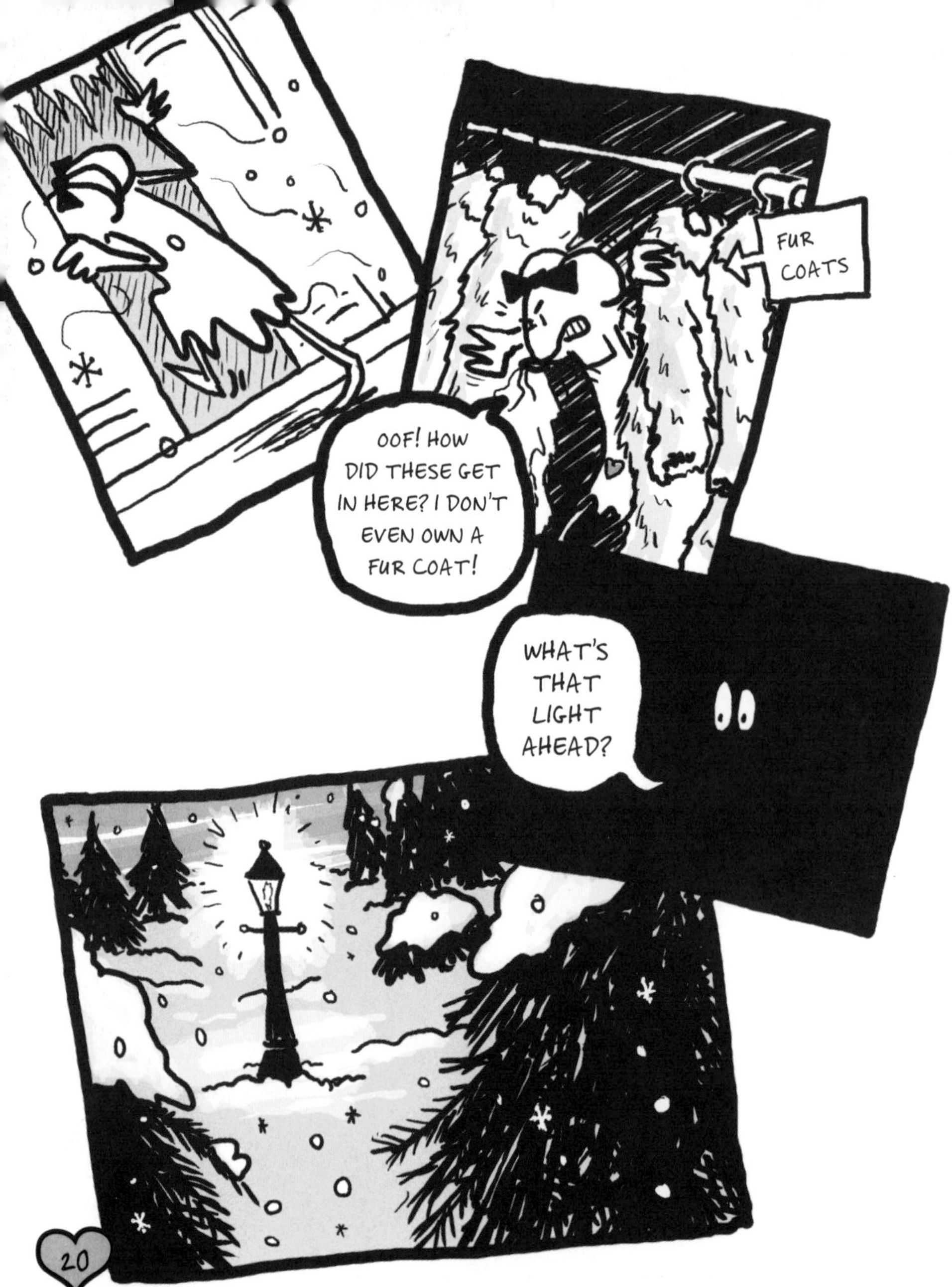
FUR COATS
OOF! HOW DID THESE GET IN HERE? I DON'T EVEN OWN A FUR COAT!
WHAT'S THAT LIGHT AHEAD?

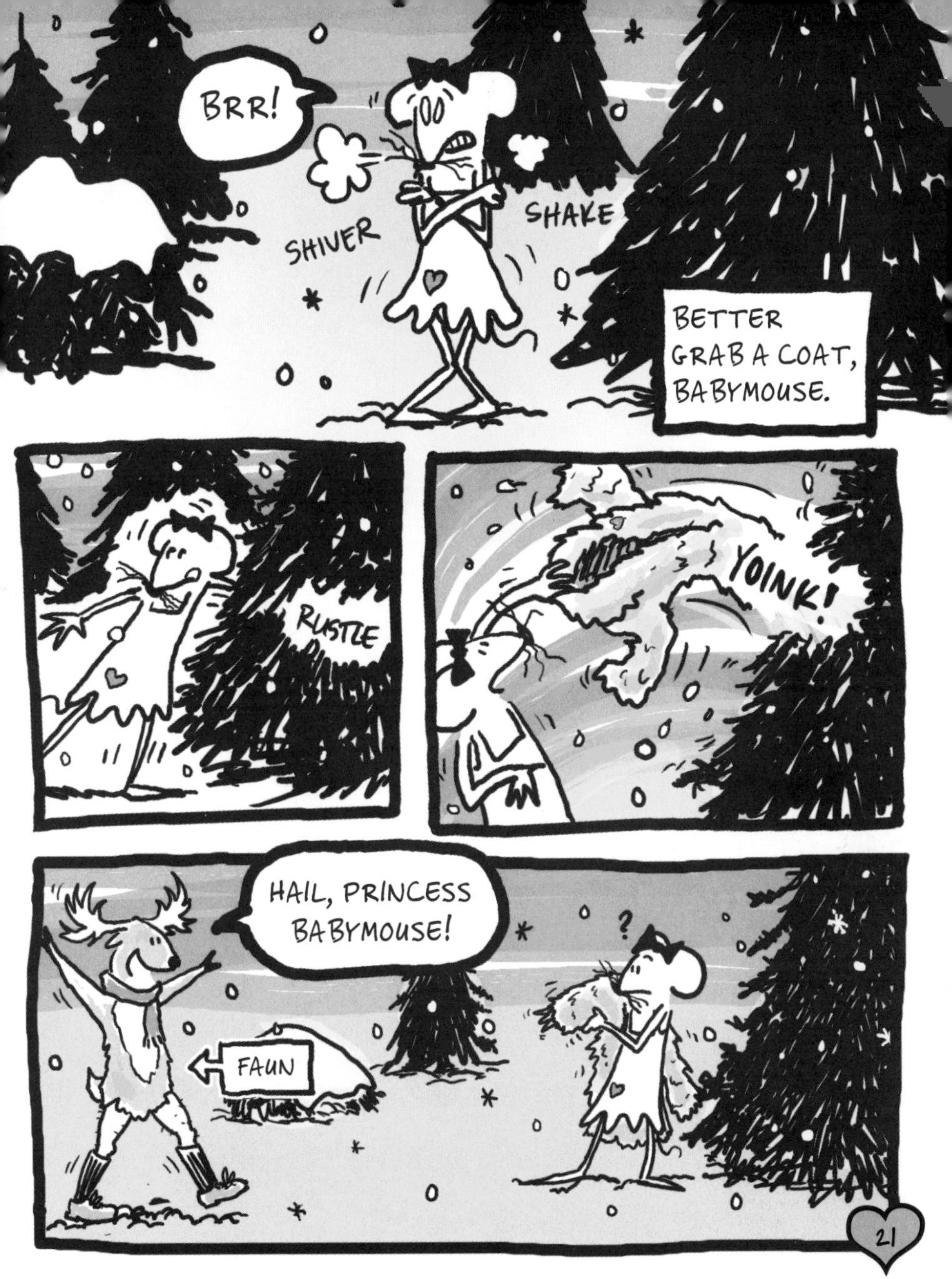
BRR!
SHIVER
SHAKE
BETTER GRAB A COAT, BABYMOUSE.
RUSTLE
YOINK!
HAIL, PRINCESS BABYMOUSE!
?
FAUN

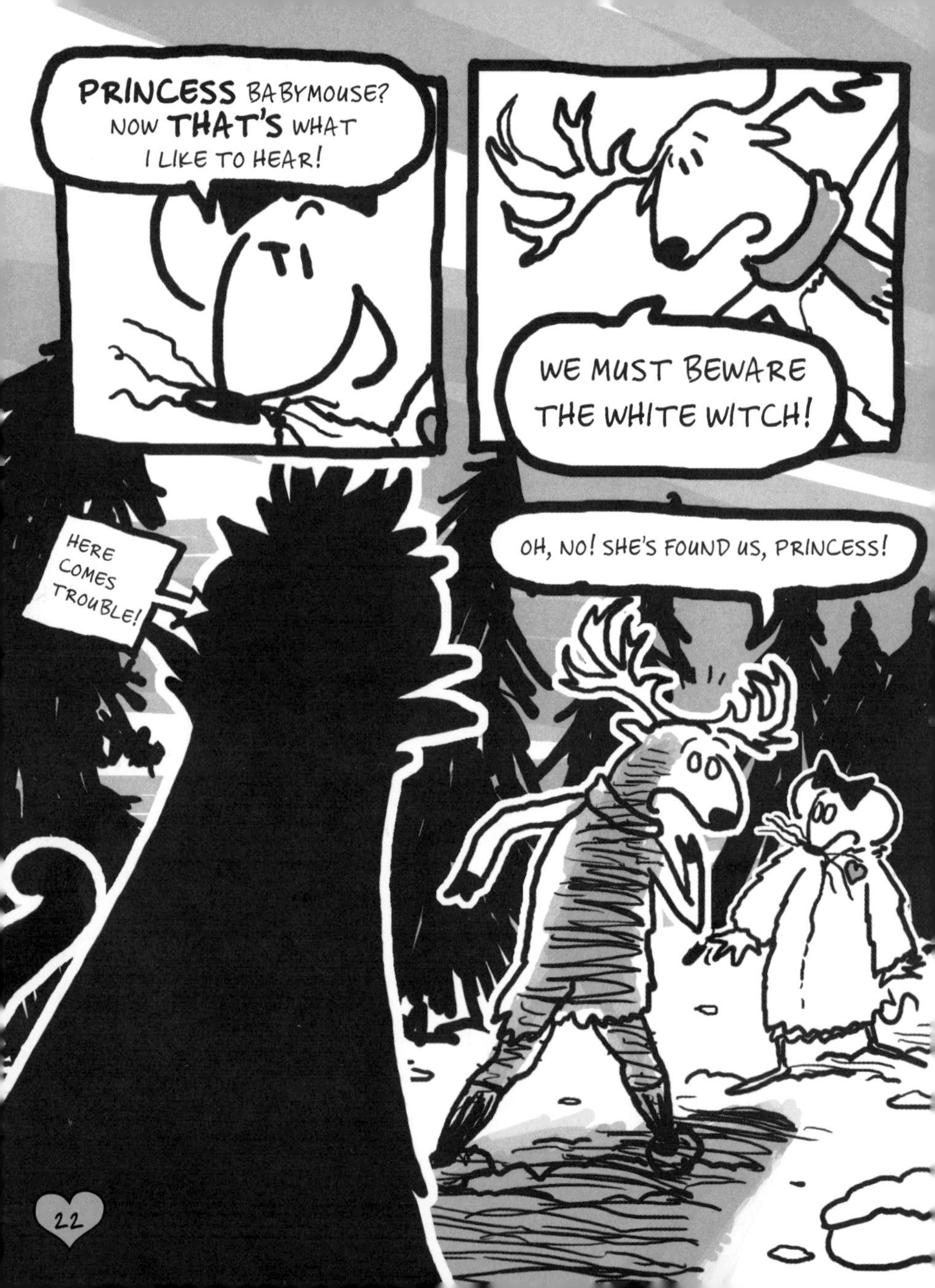
PRINCESS BABYMOUSE? NOW THAT'S WHAT I LIKE TO HEAR!
WE MUST BEWARE THE WHITE WITCH!
HERE COMES TROUBLE!
OH, NO! SHE'S FOUND US, PRINCESS!

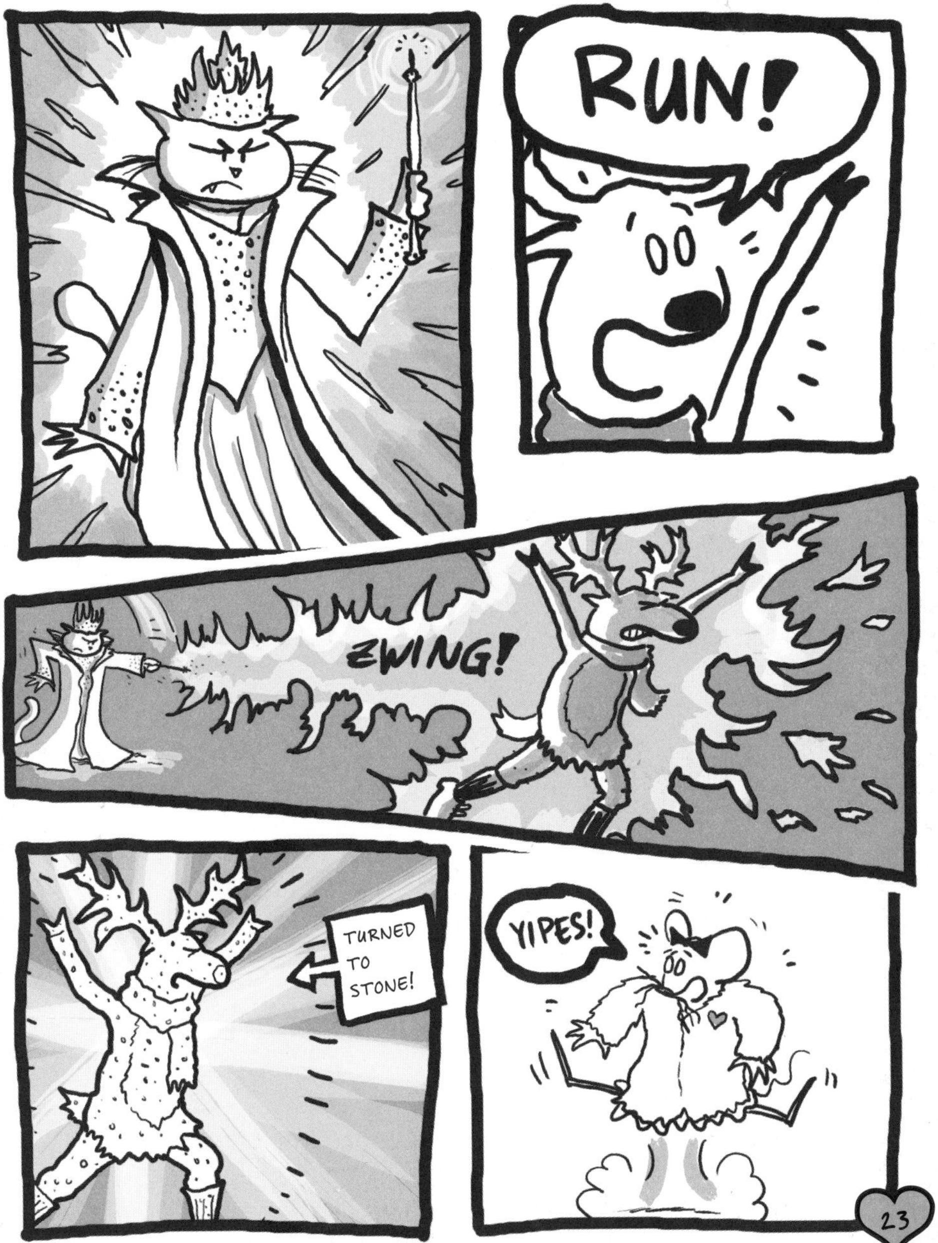
RUN!
ZWING!
TURNED TO STONE!
YIPES!

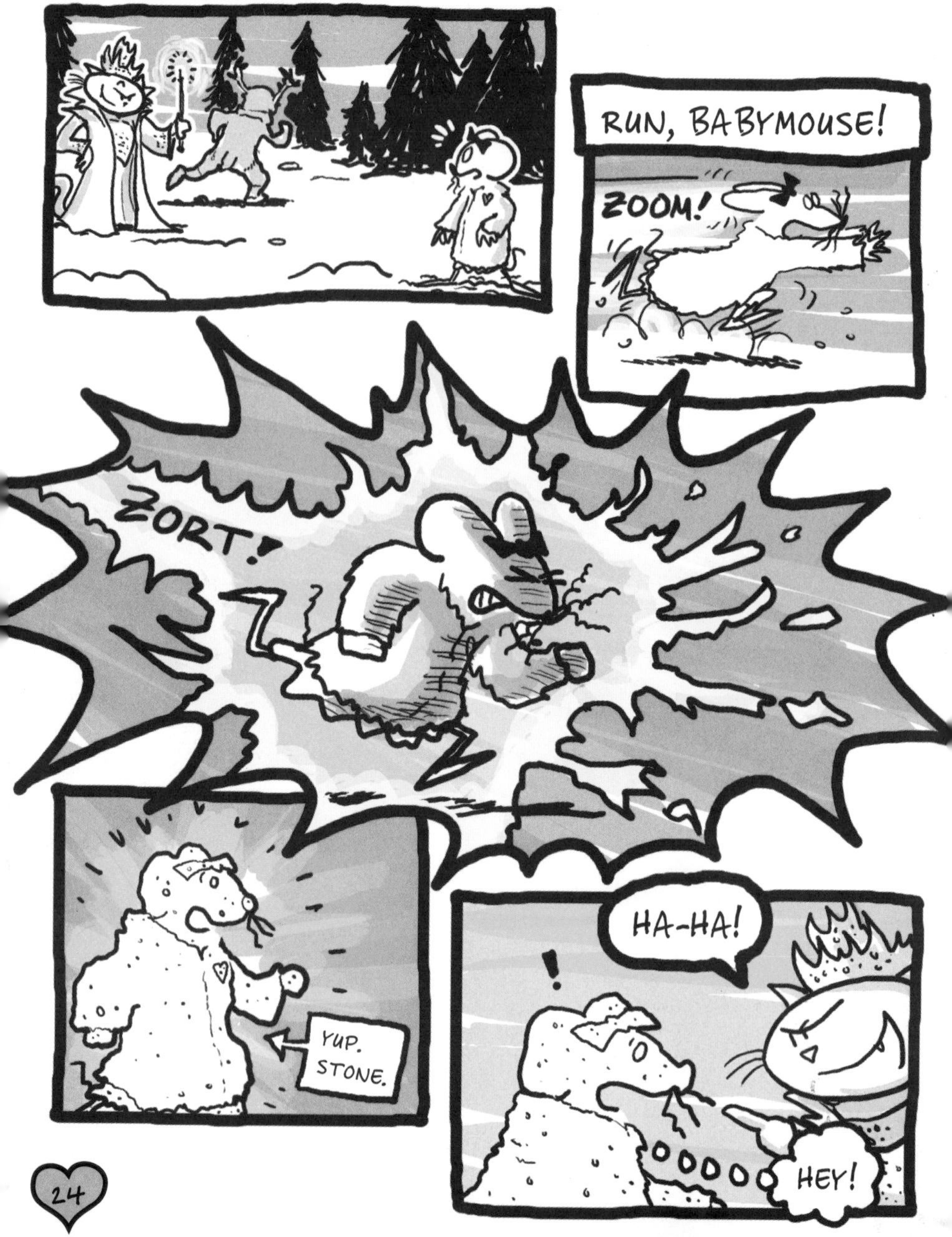
RUN, BABYMOUSE!
ZOOM!
ZORT!
YUP. STONE.
HA-HA!
!
OOOOO
HEY!

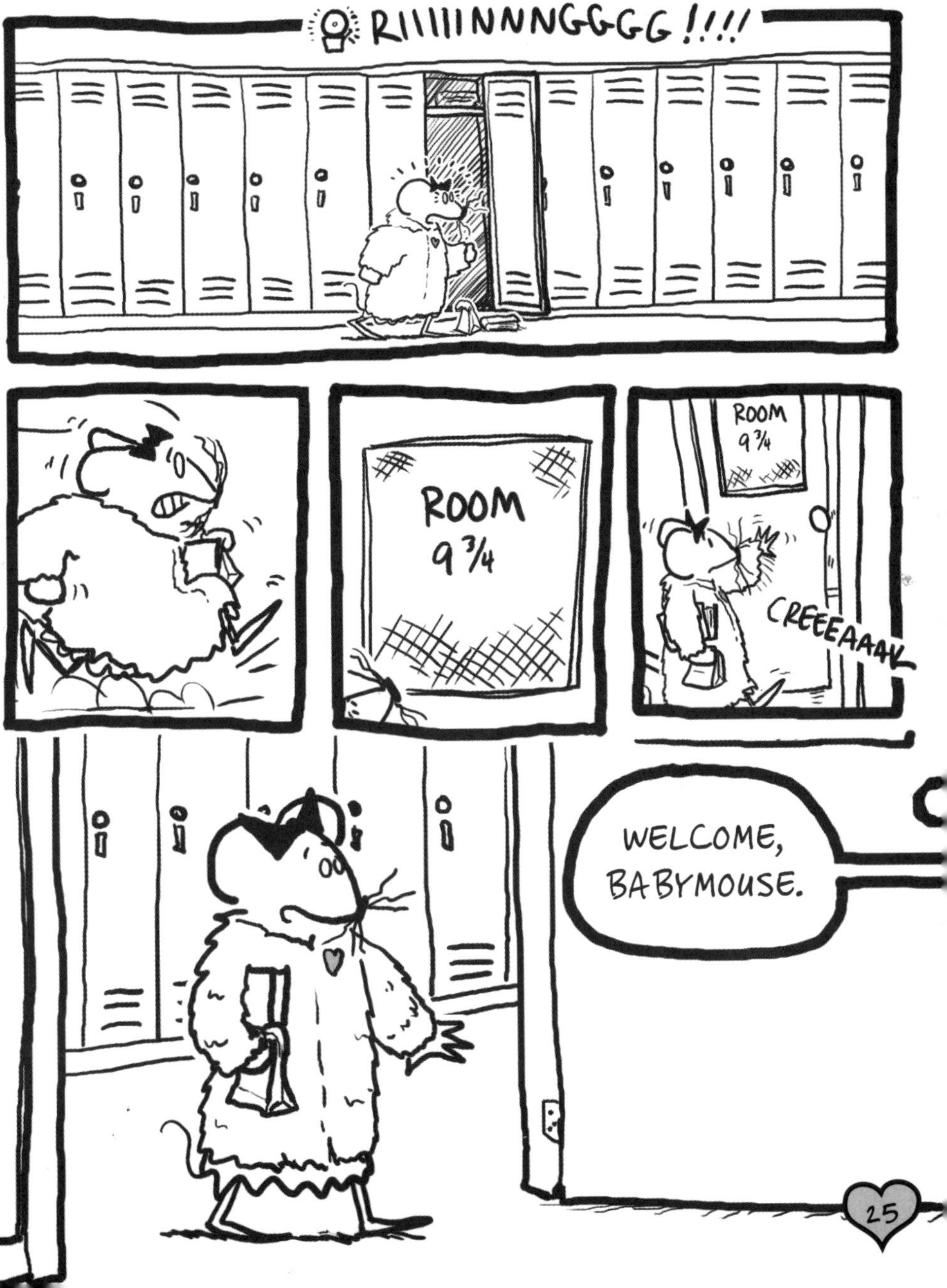
RIIIIINNNGGGG!!!!
ROOM 9 3/4
ROOM 9 3/4
CREEEAAAK
WELCOME, BABYMOUSE.

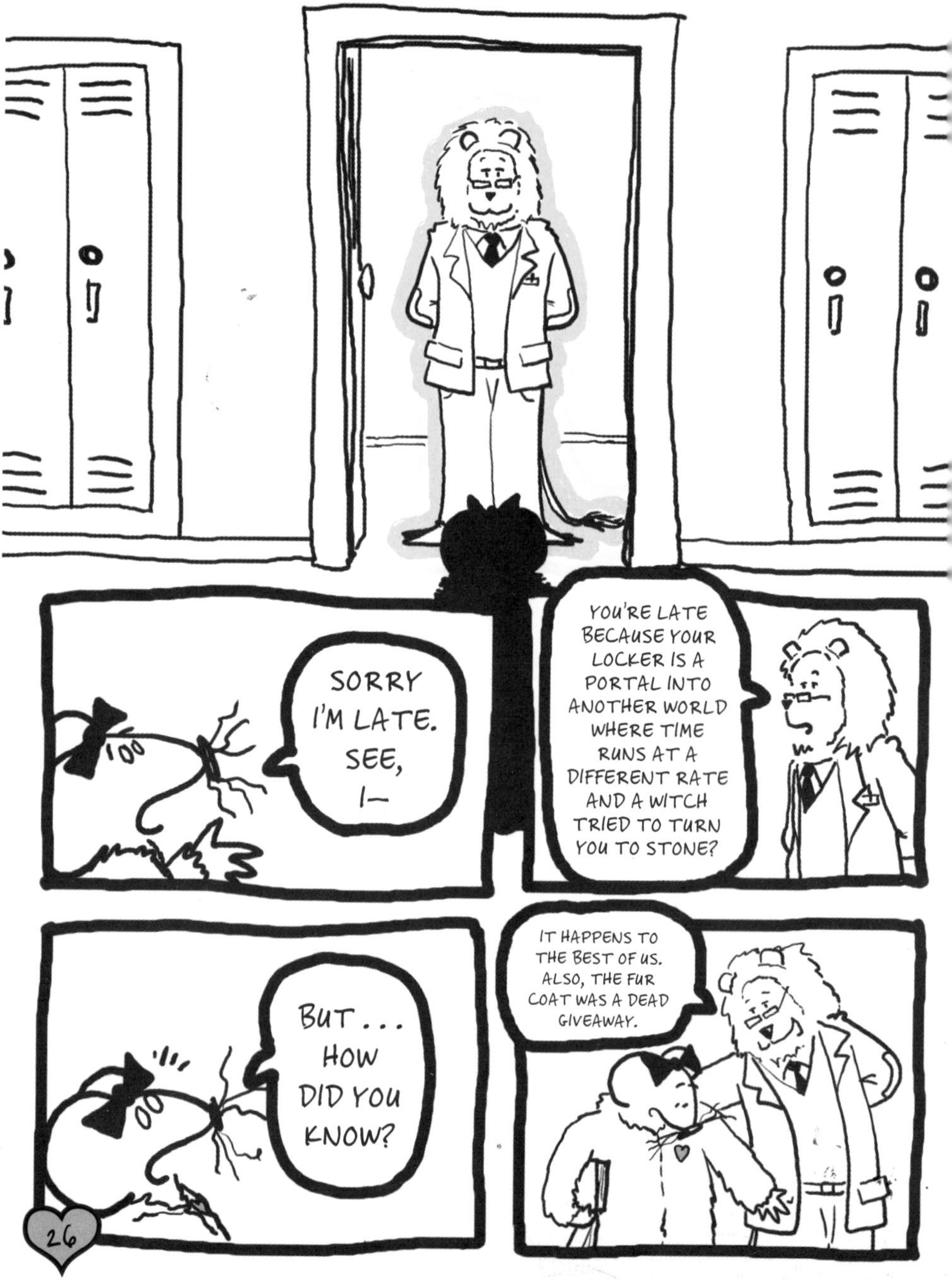
SORRY I'M LATE. SEE, I—
YOU'RE LATE BECAUSE YOUR LOCKER IS A PORTAL INTO ANOTHER WORLD WHERE TIME RUNS AT A DIFFERENT RATE AND A WITCH TRIED TO TURN YOU TO STONE?
BUT . . . HOW DID YOU KNOW?
IT HAPPENS TO THE BEST OF US. ALSO, THE FUR COAT WAS A DEAD GIVEAWAY.

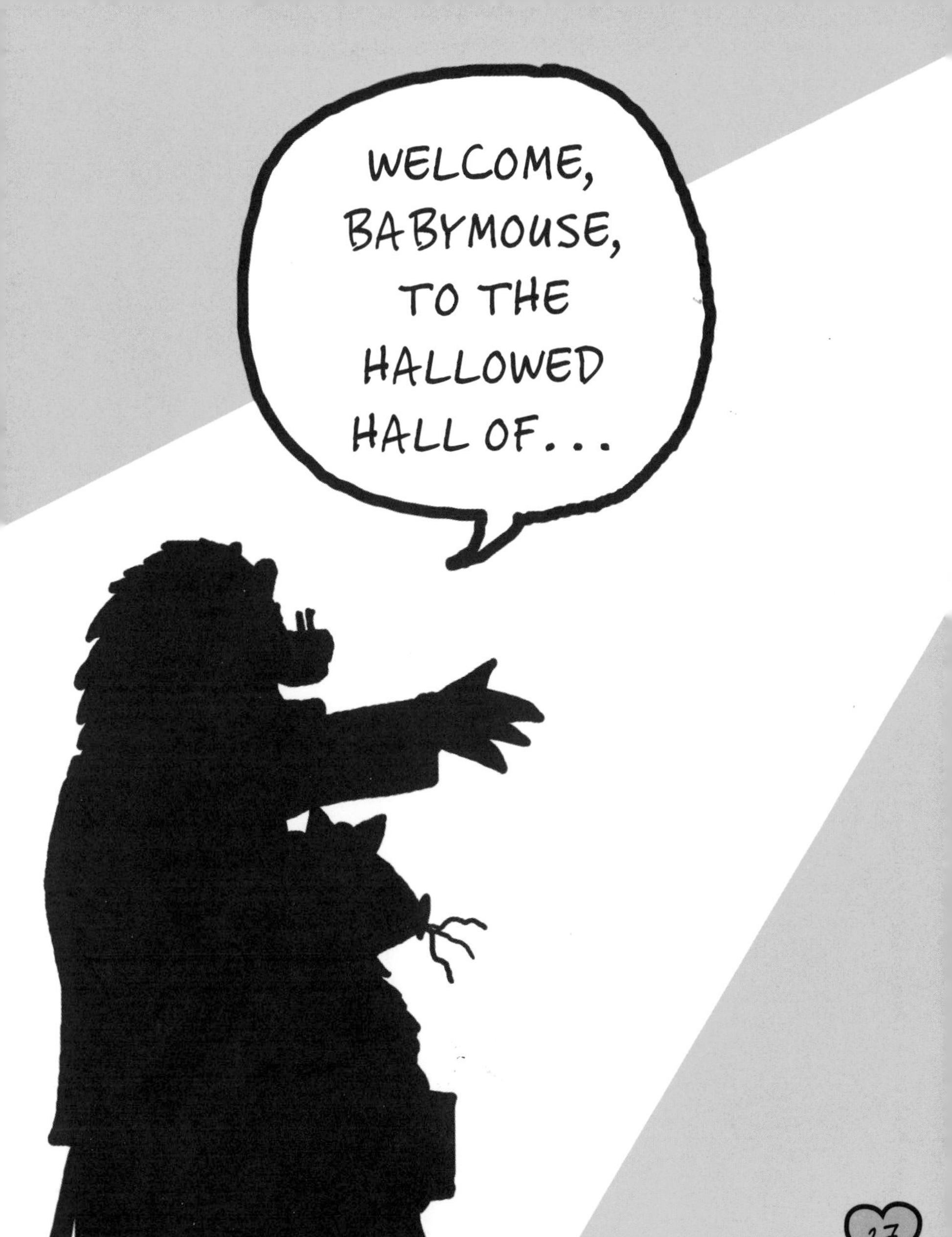
WELCOME, BABYMOUSE, TO THE HALLOWED HALL OF...

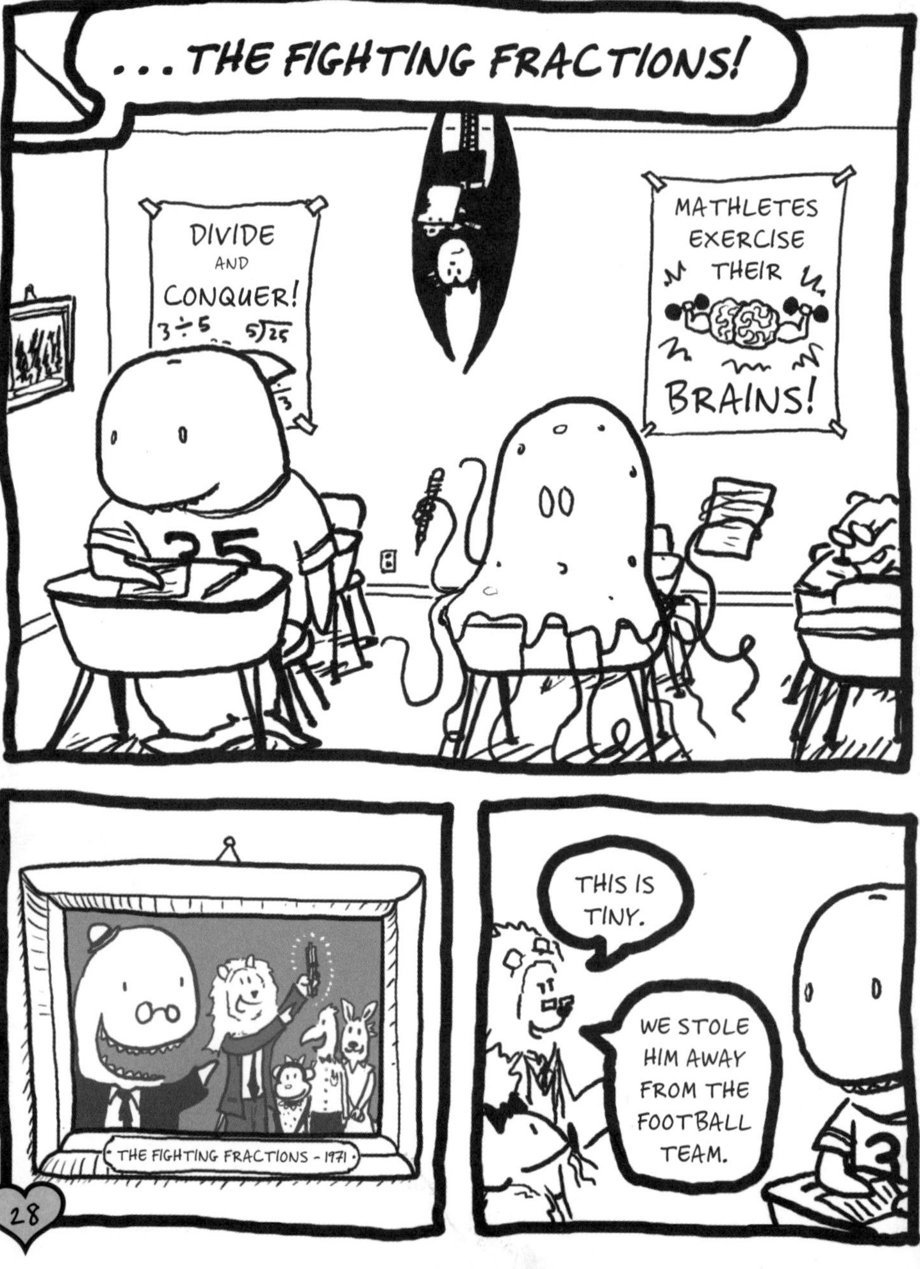
. . . THE FIGHTING FRACTIONS!
DIVIDE AND CONQUER!
3÷5
5)25
MATHLETES EXERCISE THEIR BRAINS!
25
THE FIGHTING FRACTIONS - 1971
THIS IS TINY.
WE STOLE HIM AWAY FROM THE FOOTBALL TEAM.

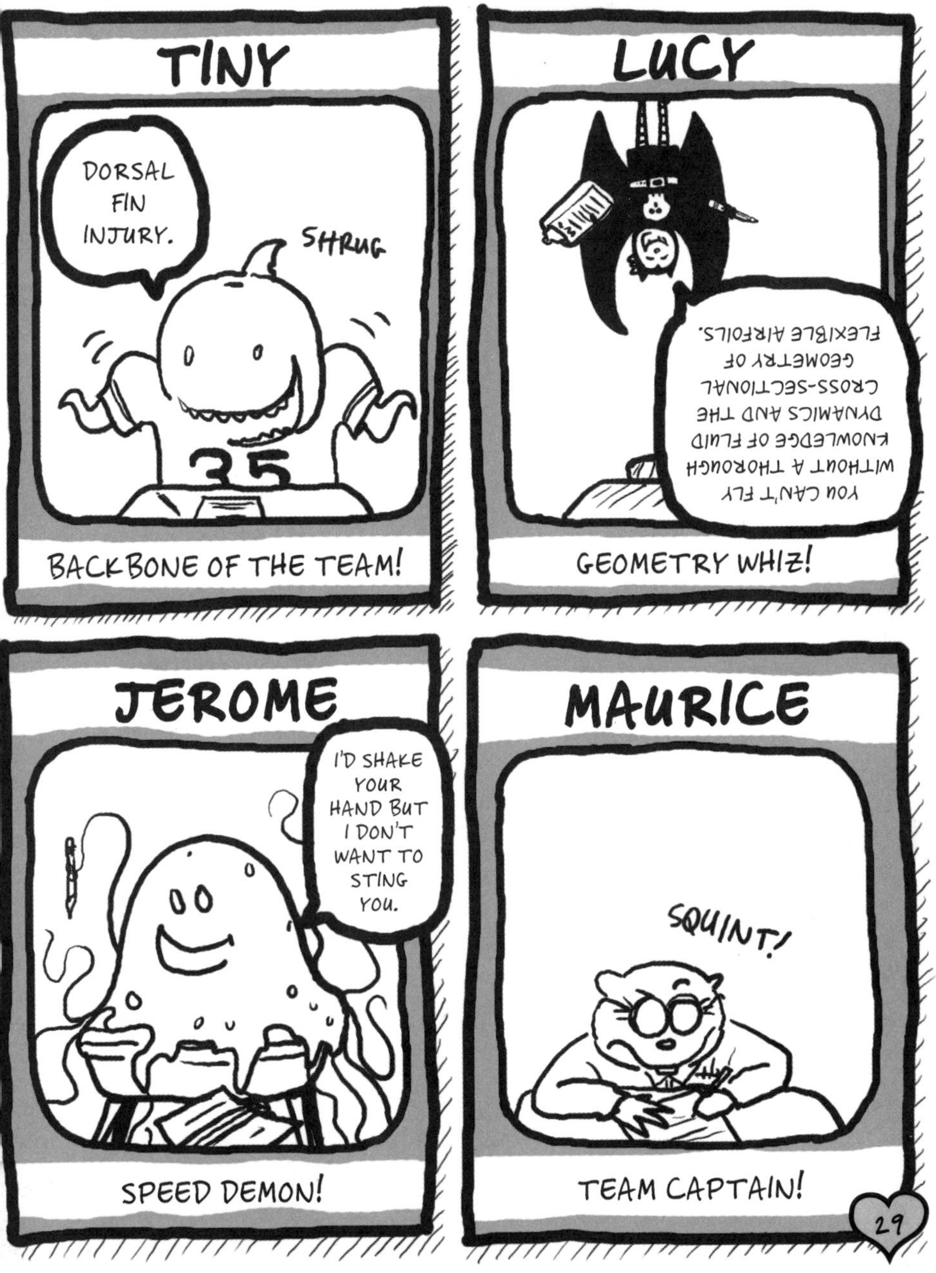
TINY
DORSAL FIN INJURY.
SHRUG
35
BACKBONE OF THE TEAM!
LUCY
YOU CAN'T FLY WITHOUT A THOROUGH KNOWLEDGE OF FLUID DYNAMICS AND THE CROSS-SECTIONAL GEOMETRY OF FLEXIBLE AIRFOILS.
GEOMETRY WHIZ!
JEROME
I'D SHAKE YOUR HAND BUT I DON'T WANT TO STING YOU.
SPEED DEMON!
MAURICE
SQUINT!
TEAM CAPTAIN!

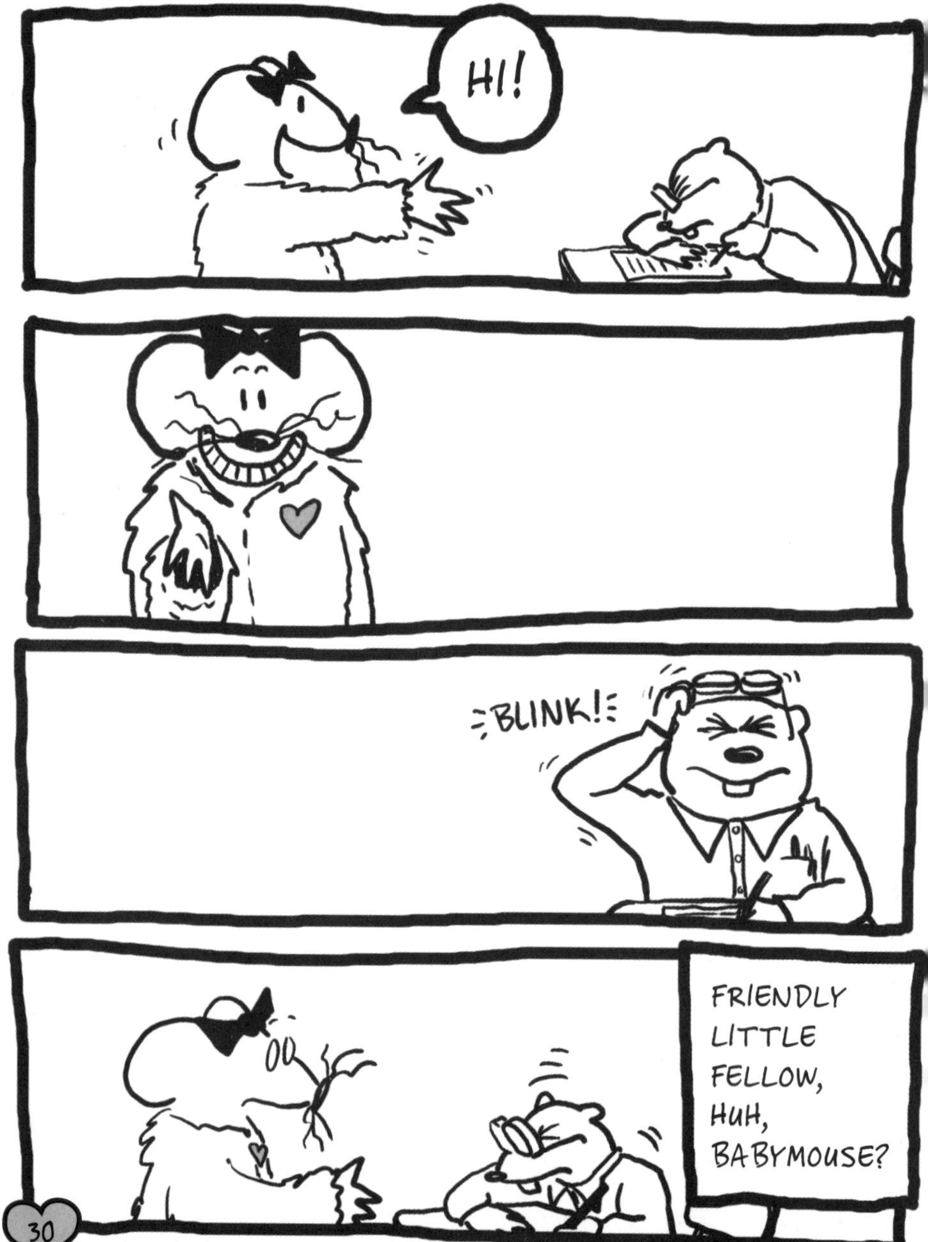
HI!
BLINK!
FRIENDLY LITTLE FELLOW, HUH, BABYMOUSE?

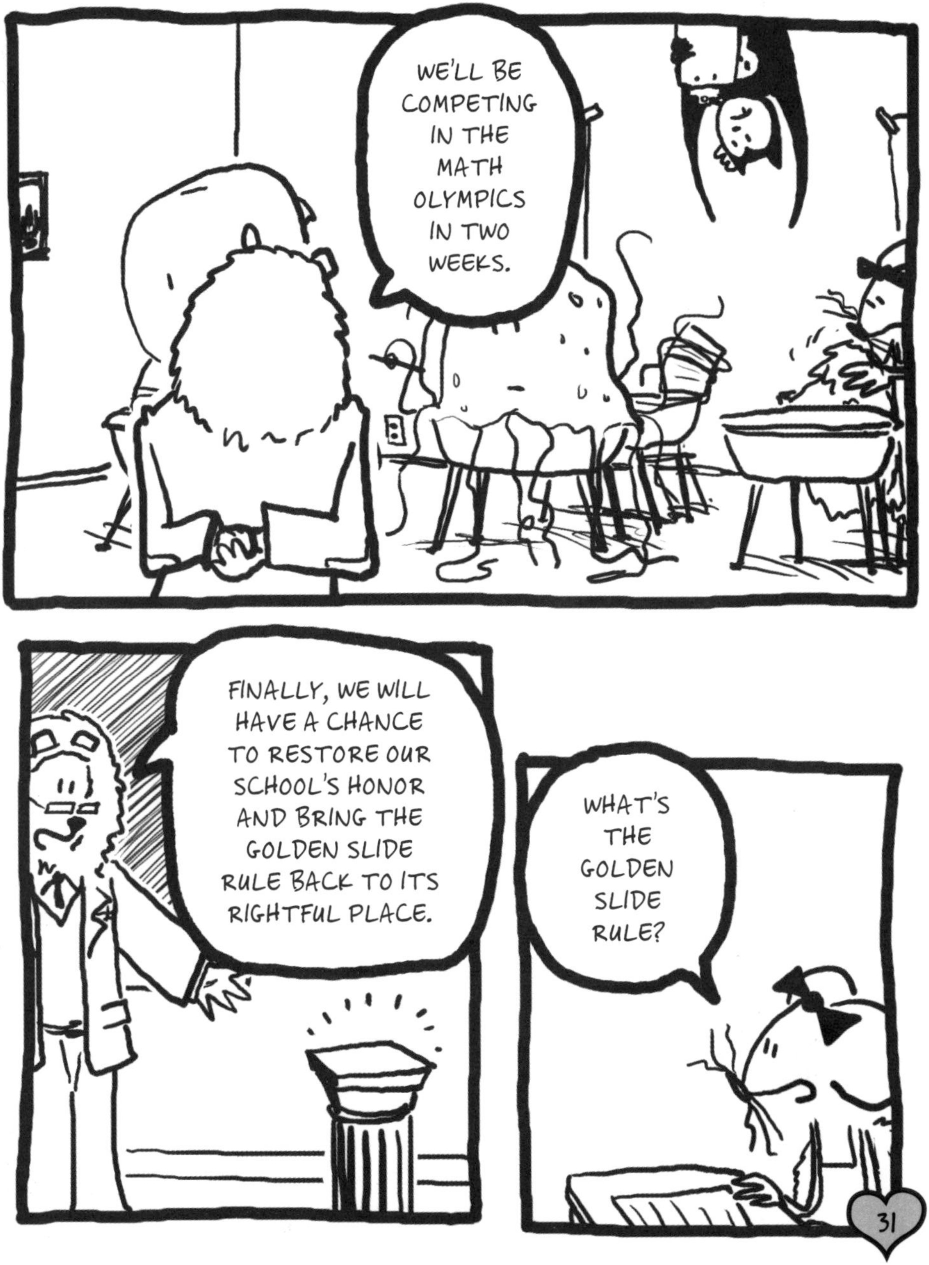
WE'LL BE COMPETING IN THE MATH OLYMPICS IN TWO WEEKS.
FINALLY, WE WILL HAVE A CHANCE TO RESTORE OUR SCHOOL'S HONOR AND BRING THE GOLDEN SLIDE RULE BACK TO ITS RIGHTFUL PLACE.
WHAT'S THE GOLDEN SLIDE RULE?

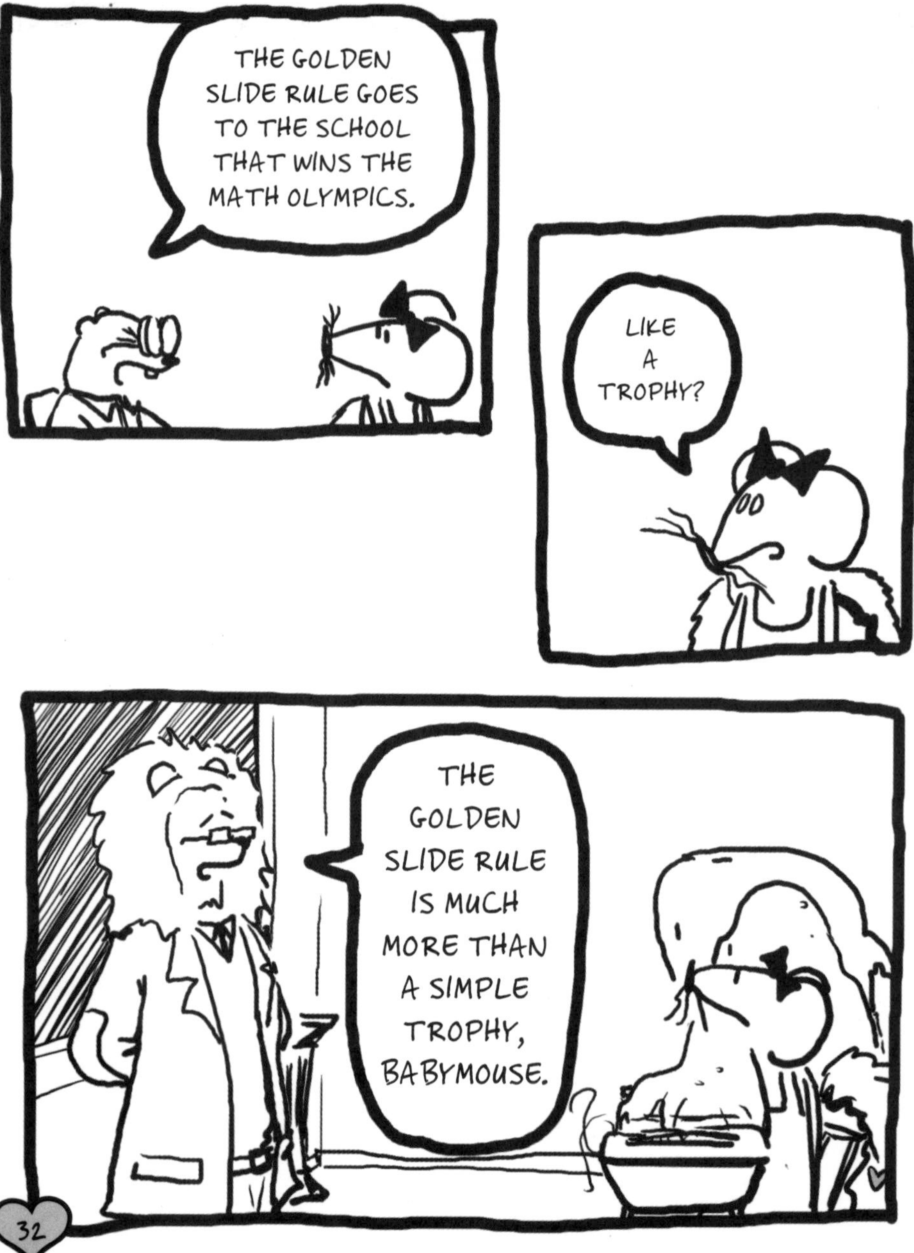
THE GOLDEN SLIDE RULE GOES TO THE SCHOOL THAT WINS THE MATH OLYMPICS.
LIKE A TROPHY?
THE GOLDEN SLIDE RULE IS MUCH MORE THAN A SIMPLE TROPHY, BABYMOUSE.

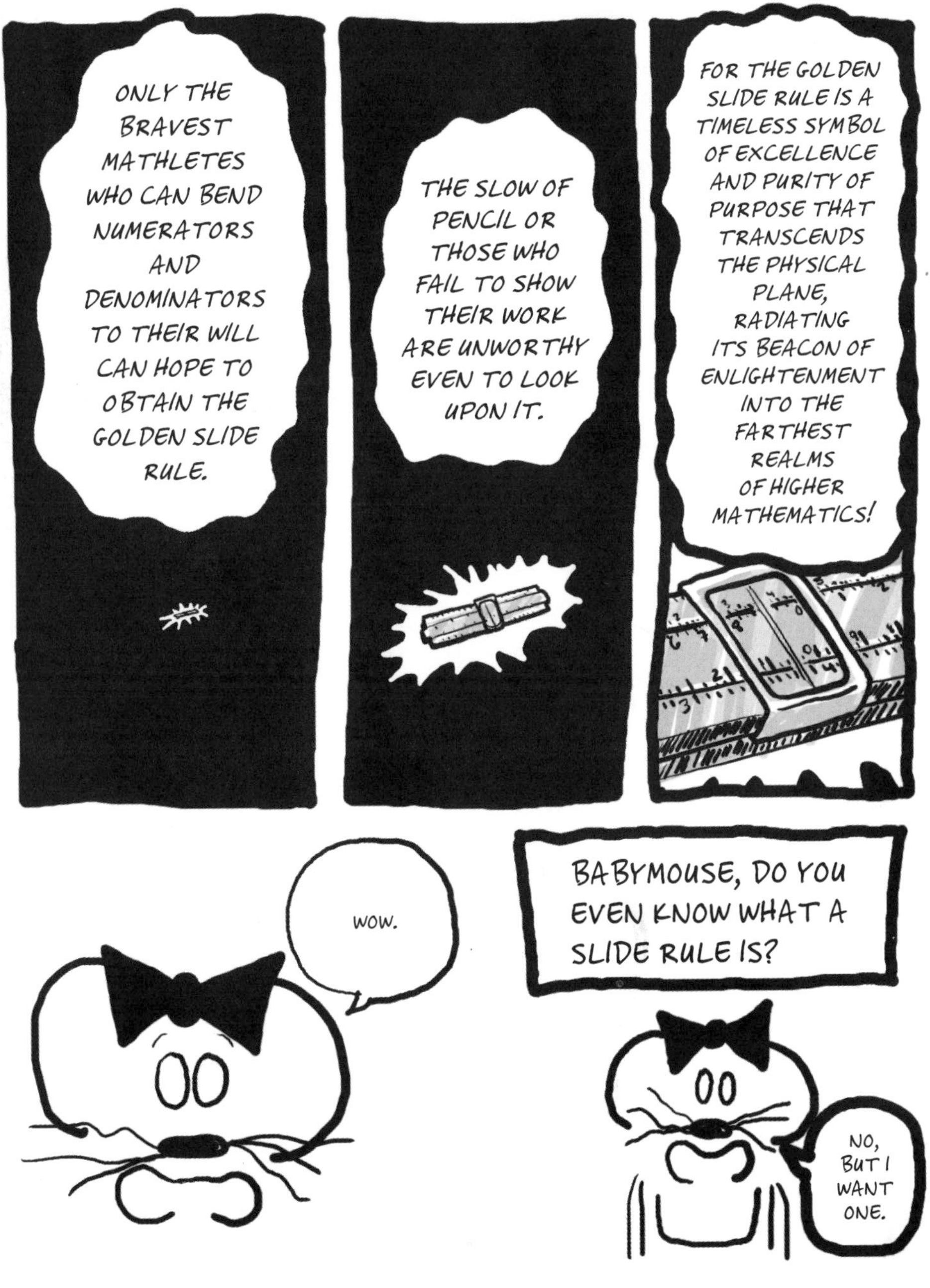
ONLY THE BRAVEST MATHLETES WHO CAN BEND NUMERATORS AND DENOMINATORS TO THEIR WILL CAN HOPE TO OBTAIN THE GOLDEN SLIDE RULE.
THE SLOW OF PENCIL OR THOSE WHO FAIL TO SHOW THEIR WORK ARE UNWORTHY EVEN TO LOOK UPON IT.
FOR THE GOLDEN SLIDE RULE IS A TIMELESS SYMBOL OF EXCELLENCE AND PURITY OF PURPOSE THAT TRANSCENDS THE PHYSICAL PLANE, RADIATING ITS BEACON OF ENLIGHTENMENT INTO THE FARTHEST REALMS OF HIGHER MATHEMATICS!
WOW.
BABYMOUSE, DO YOU EVEN KNOW WHAT A SLIDE RULE IS?
NO, BUT I WANT ONE.

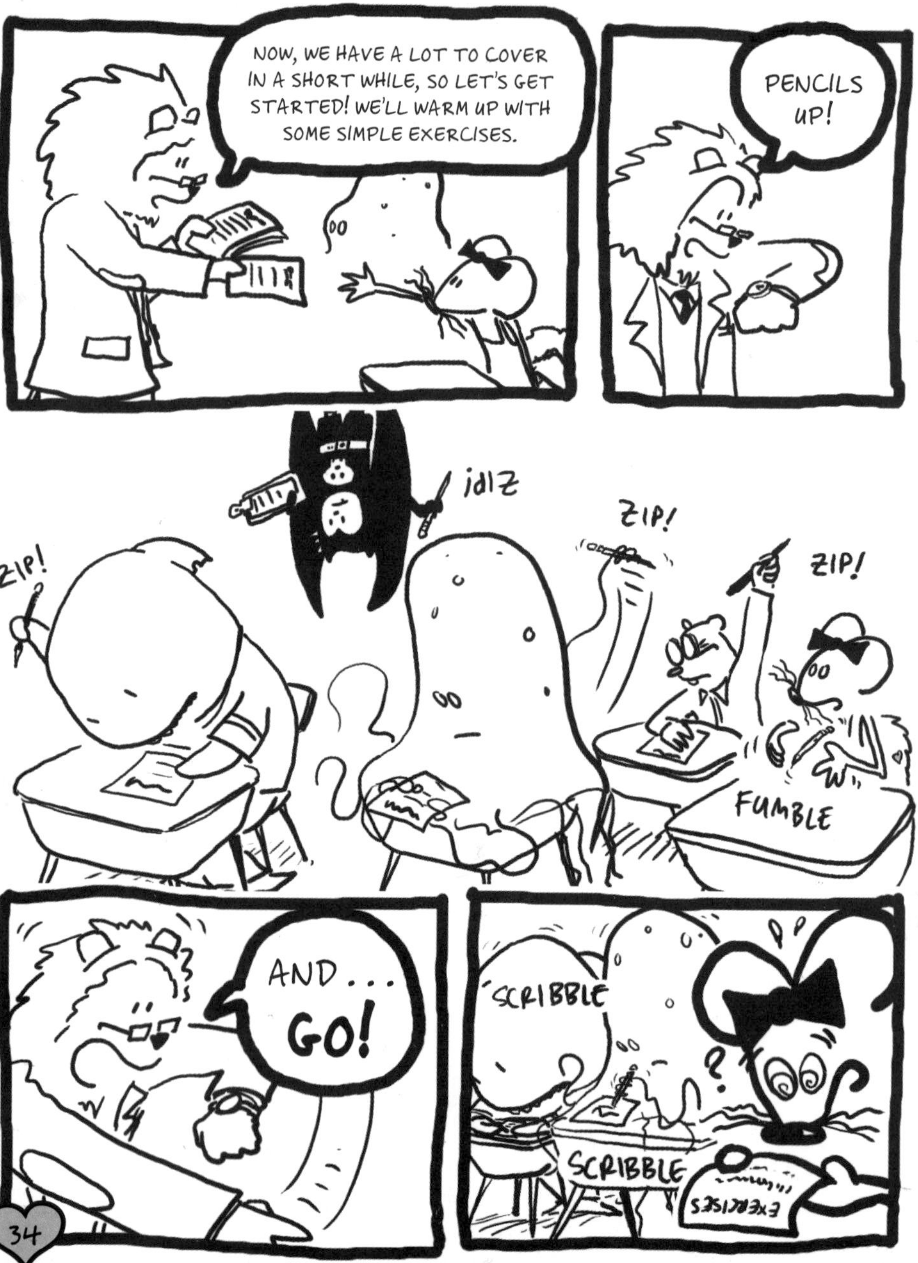
NOW, WE HAVE A LOT TO COVER IN A SHORT WHILE, SO LET'S GET STARTED! WE'LL WARM UP WITH SOME SIMPLE EXERCISES.
PENCILS UP!
ZIP!
ZIP!
ZIP!
ZIP!
FUMBLE
AND . . .
GO!
SCRIBBLE
SCRIBBLE
EXERCISES

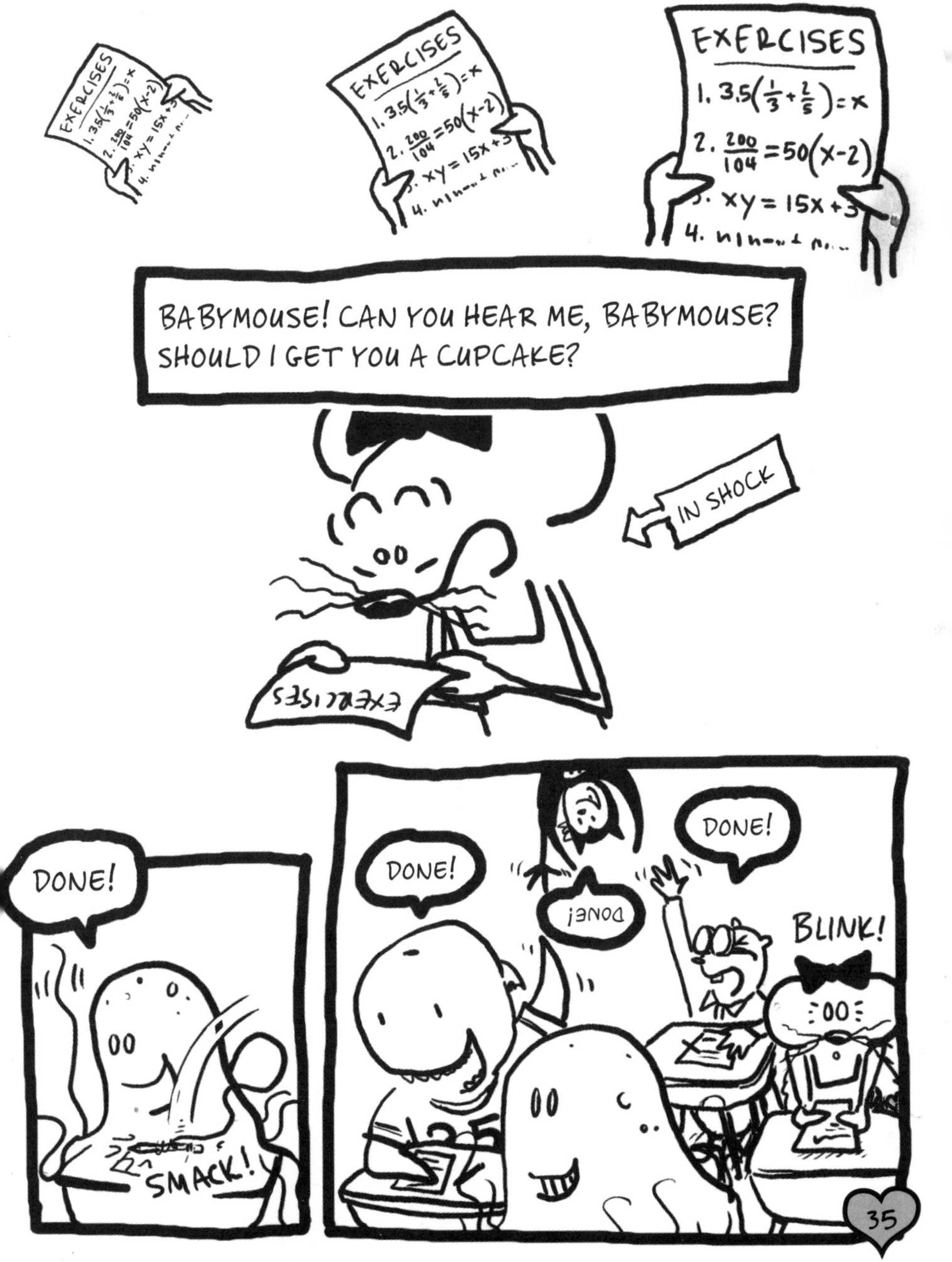
EXERCISES
EXERCISES
EXERCISES
1. 3.5(1/3 + 2/5) = x
2. 200/104 = 50(x-2)
xy = 15x + 3
BABYMOUSE! CAN YOU HEAR ME, BABYMOUSE? SHOULD I GET YOU A CUPCAKE?
IN SHOCK
EXERCISES
DONE!
SMACK!
DONE!
DONE!
DONE!
BLINK!

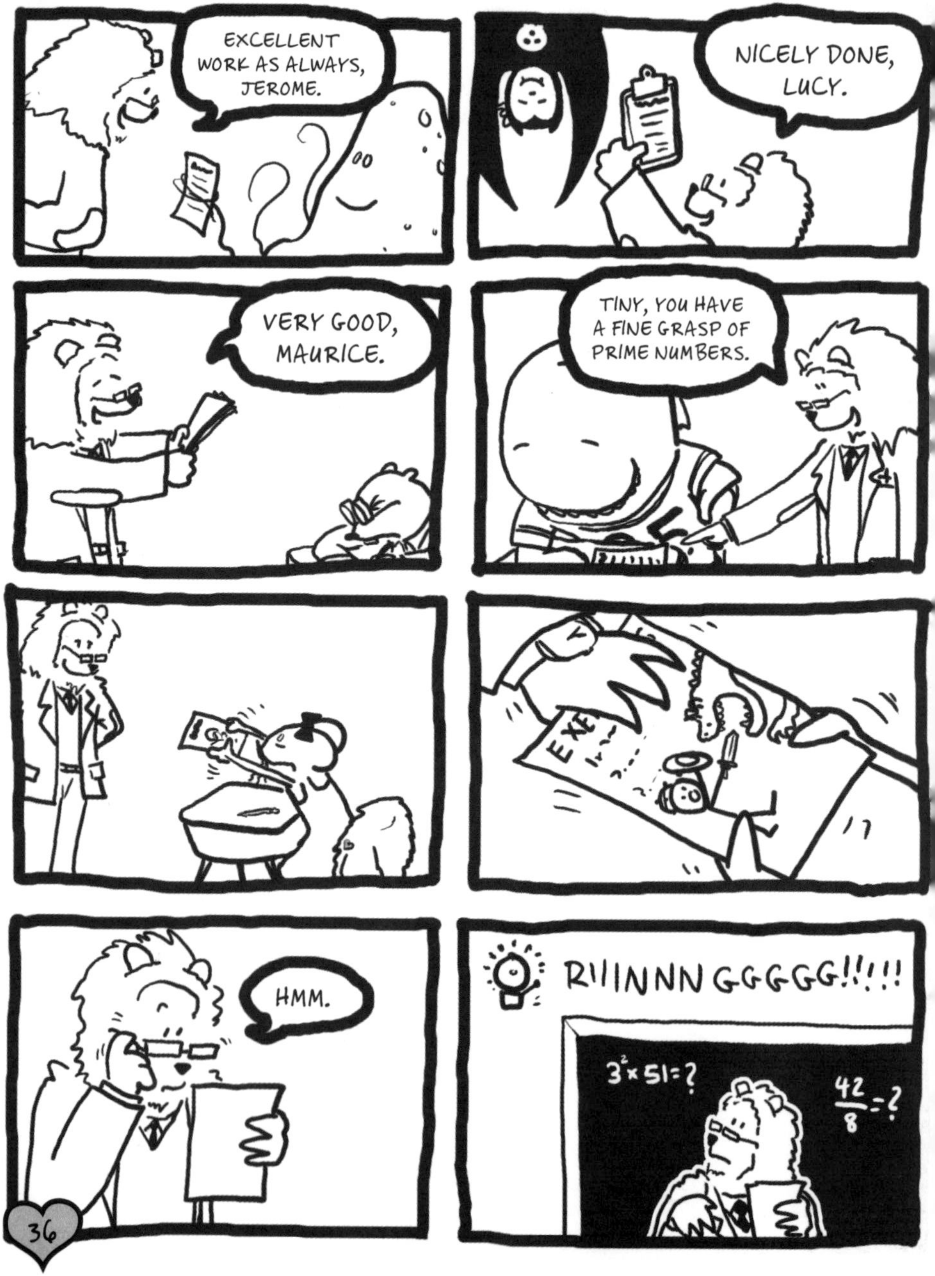
EXCELLENT WORK AS ALWAYS, JEROME.
NICELY DONE, LUCY.
VERY GOOD, MAURICE.
TINY, YOU HAVE A FINE GRASP OF PRIME NUMBERS.
HMM.
RIIINNNGGGGG!!!!!
$3^2 \times 51 = ?$
$\frac{42}{8} = ?$

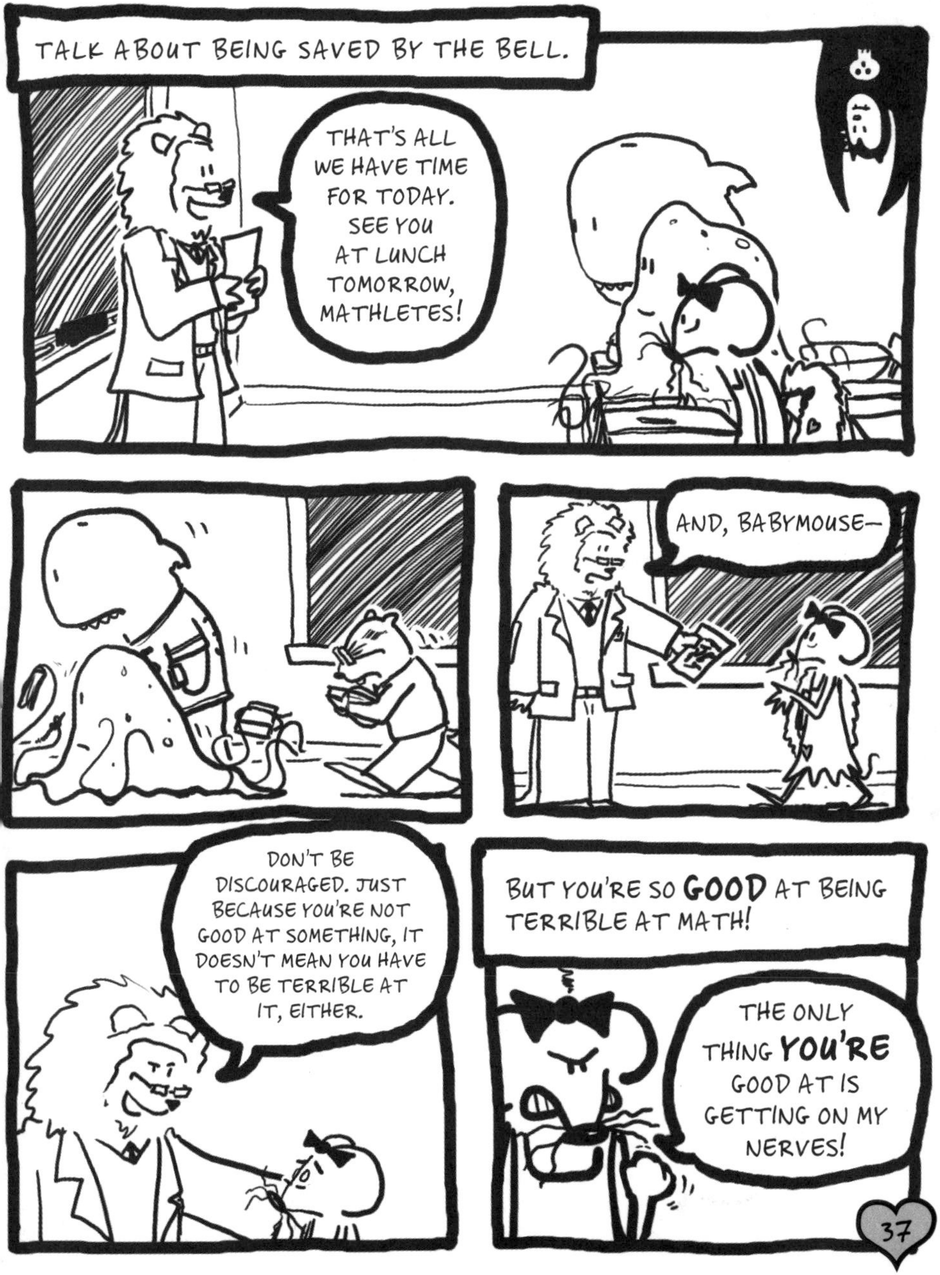
TALK ABOUT BEING SAVED BY THE BELL.
THAT'S ALL WE HAVE TIME FOR TODAY. SEE YOU AT LUNCH TOMORROW, MATHLETES!
AND, BABYMOUSE—
DON'T BE DISCOURAGED. JUST BECAUSE YOU'RE NOT GOOD AT SOMETHING, IT DOESN'T MEAN YOU HAVE TO BE TERRIBLE AT IT, EITHER.
BUT YOU'RE SO **GOOD** AT BEING TERRIBLE AT MATH!
THE ONLY THING **YOU'RE** GOOD AT IS GETTING ON MY NERVES!

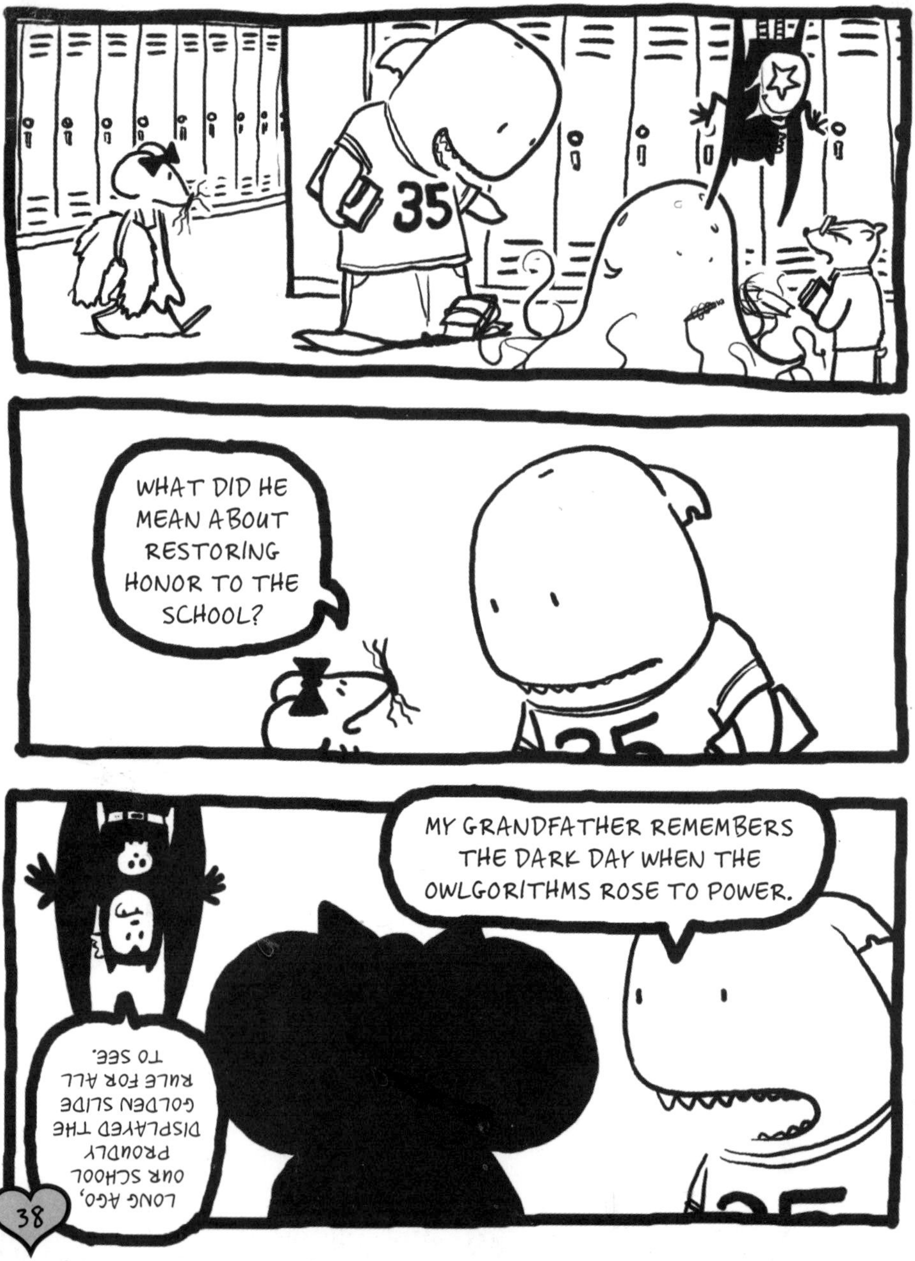
WHAT DID HE MEAN ABOUT RESTORING HONOR TO THE SCHOOL?
MY GRANDFATHER REMEMBERS THE DARK DAY WHEN THE OWLGORITHMS ROSE TO POWER.
LONG AGO, OUR SCHOOL PROUDLY DISPLAYED THE GOLDEN SLIDE RULE FOR ALL TO SEE.

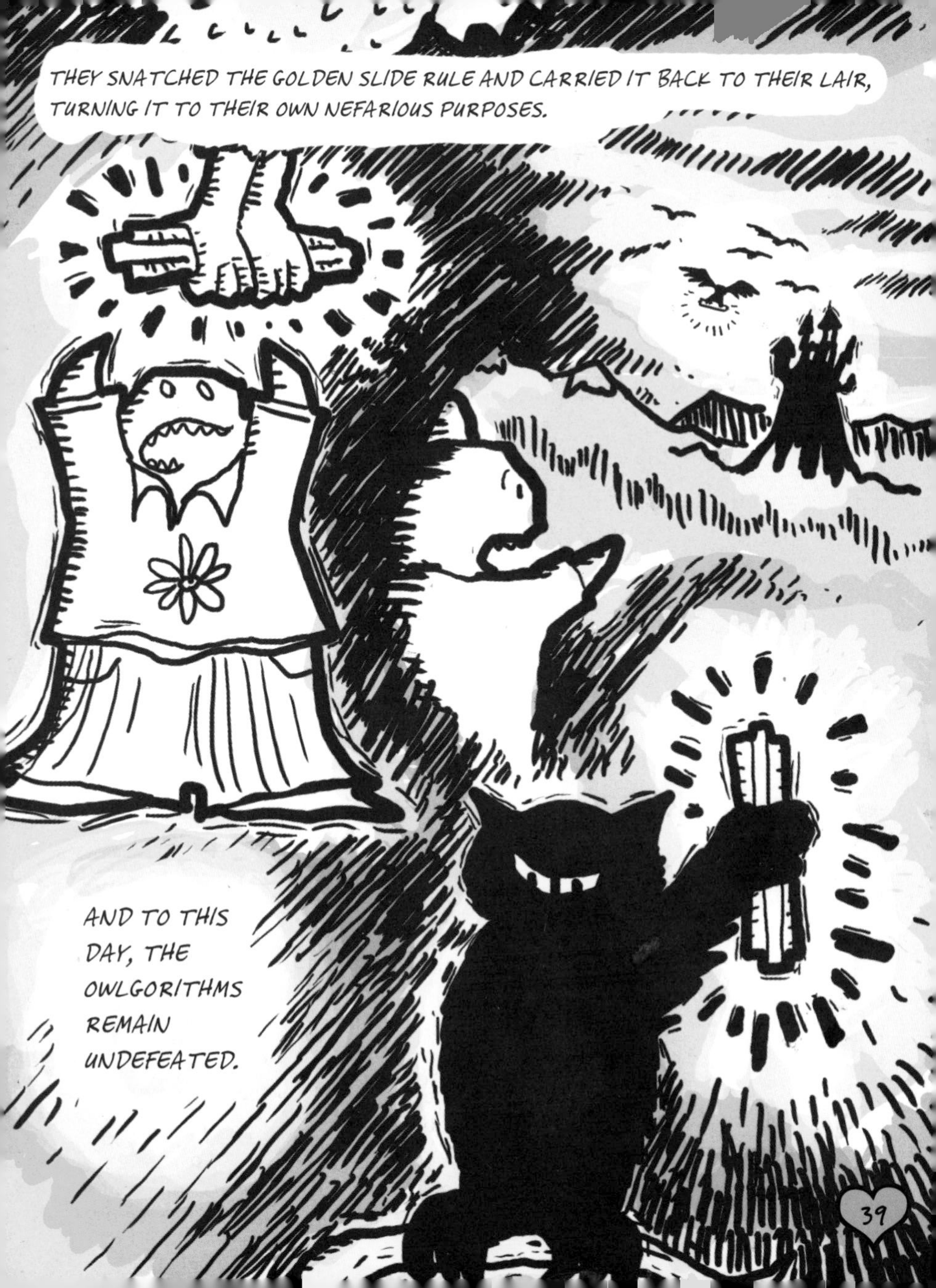
THEY SNATCHED THE GOLDEN SLIDE RULE AND CARRIED IT BACK TO THEIR LAIR, TURNING IT TO THEIR OWN NEFARIOUS PURPOSES.
AND TO THIS DAY, THE OWLGORITHMS REMAIN UNDEFEATED.

BUT THERE IS A PROPHECY THAT ONE WILL COME, A GIFTED ONE WITH A TRUE HEART, WHO WILL LEAD THE FIGHTING FRACTIONS TO GLORY AND RESTORE THE GOLDEN SLIDE RULE TO ITS RIGHTFUL HOME.

ARE YOU THE ONE THEY SPEAK OF?

UH...

EXERCISES

35

THAT WOULD BE A NO.

THE OWLGORITHMS ARE GOING TO EAT US ALIVE.

PRETTY RICH FANTASY LIFE FOR KIDS WHO DO ARITHMETIC FOR FUN, HUH, BABYMOUSE?

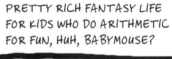

SIGH.

35

THE NEXT DAY AT LUNCHTIME.

...SO YOU SEE, THE LENGTH OF THE SUBTENDING ARC CORRESPONDS TO THE COSINE OF THE BLAH BLAH BLAH BLAH...

NOD NOD

OON

NOD

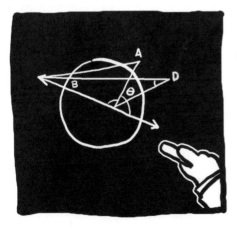

A
B
D
Θ

EYES GLAZING OVER

NOTES

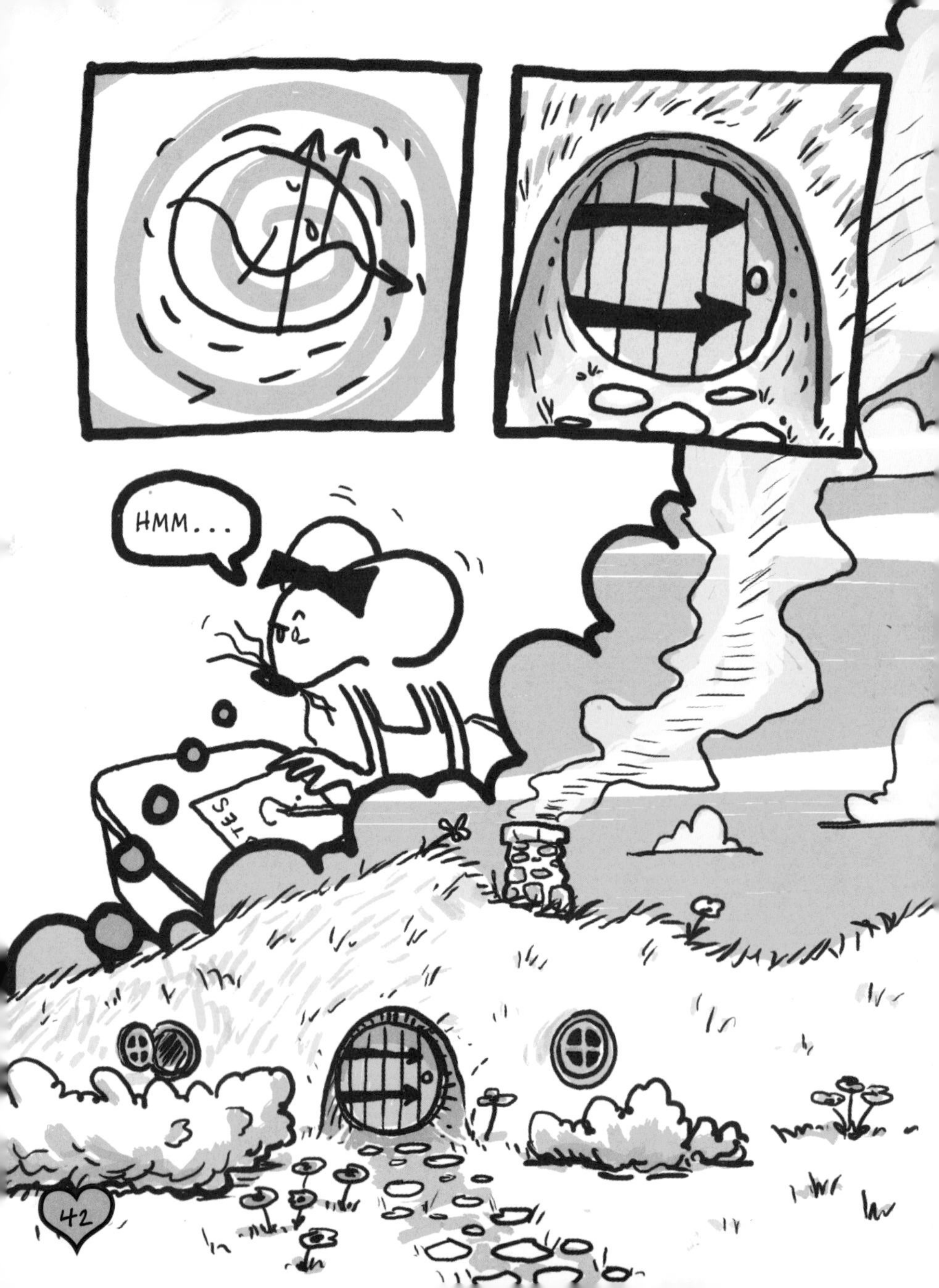
HMM...

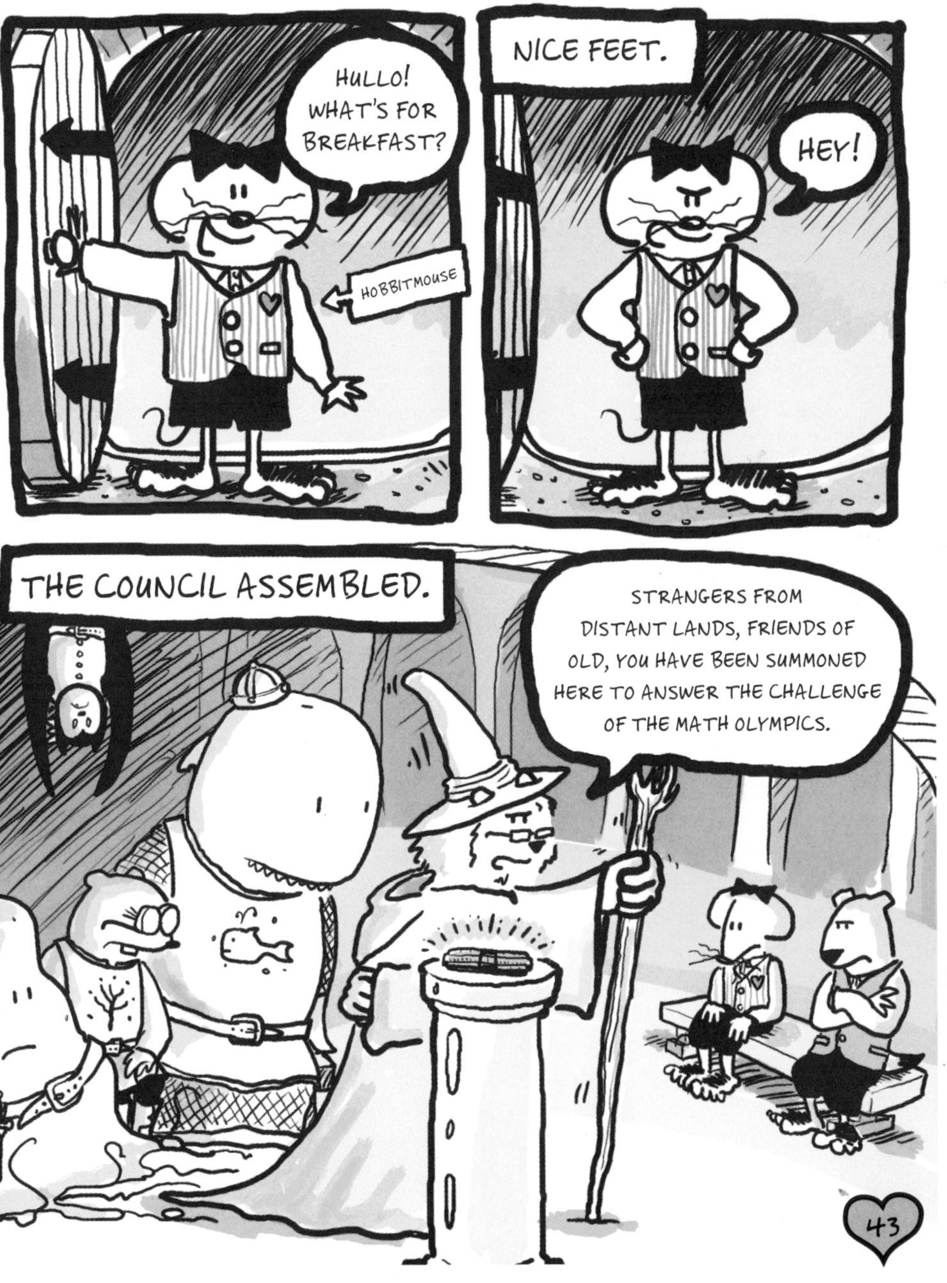
HULLO! WHAT'S FOR BREAKFAST?
HOBBITMOUSE
NICE FEET.
HEY!
THE COUNCIL ASSEMBLED.
STRANGERS FROM DISTANT LANDS, FRIENDS OF OLD, YOU HAVE BEEN SUMMONED HERE TO ANSWER THE CHALLENGE OF THE MATH OLYMPICS.

One slide to rule them all

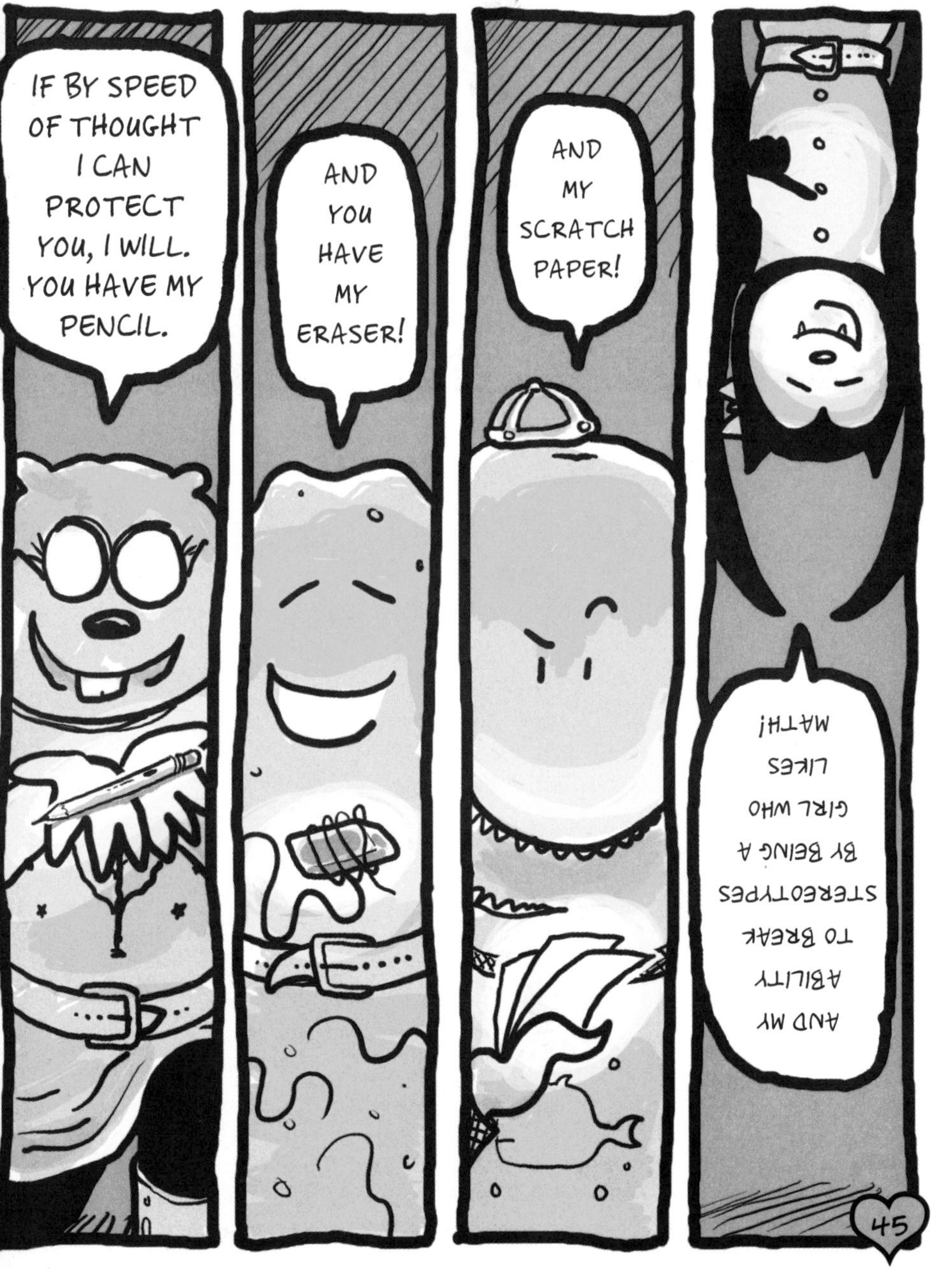
IF BY SPEED OF THOUGHT I CAN PROTECT YOU, I WILL. YOU HAVE MY PENCIL.
AND YOU HAVE MY ERASER!
AND MY SCRATCH PAPER!
AND MY ABILITY TO BREAK STEREOTYPES BY BEING A GIRL WHO LIKES MATH!

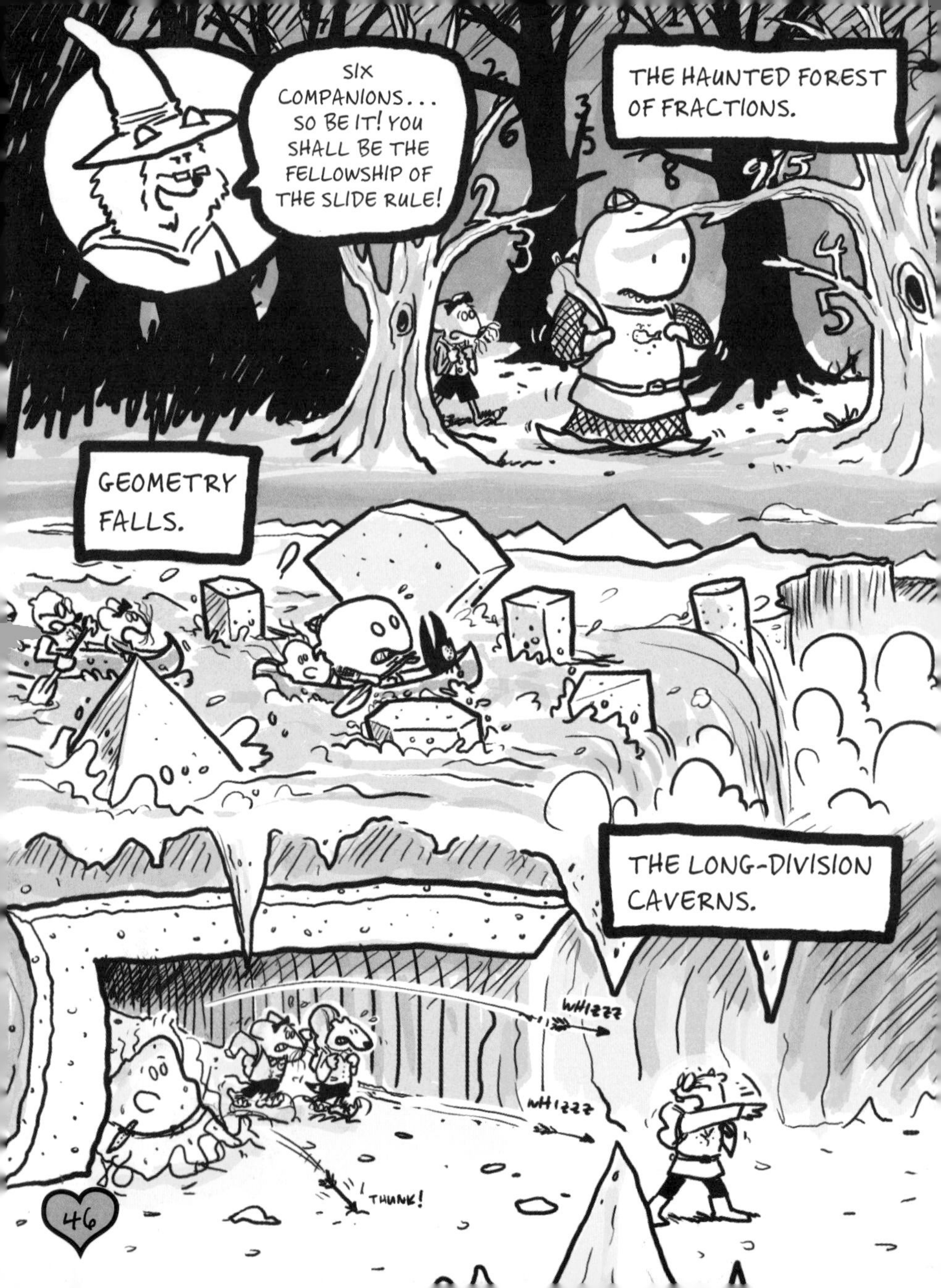
SIX COMPANIONS... SO BE IT! YOU SHALL BE THE FELLOWSHIP OF THE SLIDE RULE!
THE HAUNTED FOREST OF FRACTIONS.
GEOMETRY FALLS.
THE LONG-DIVISION CAVERNS.
WHIZZZ
WHIZZZ
THUNK!

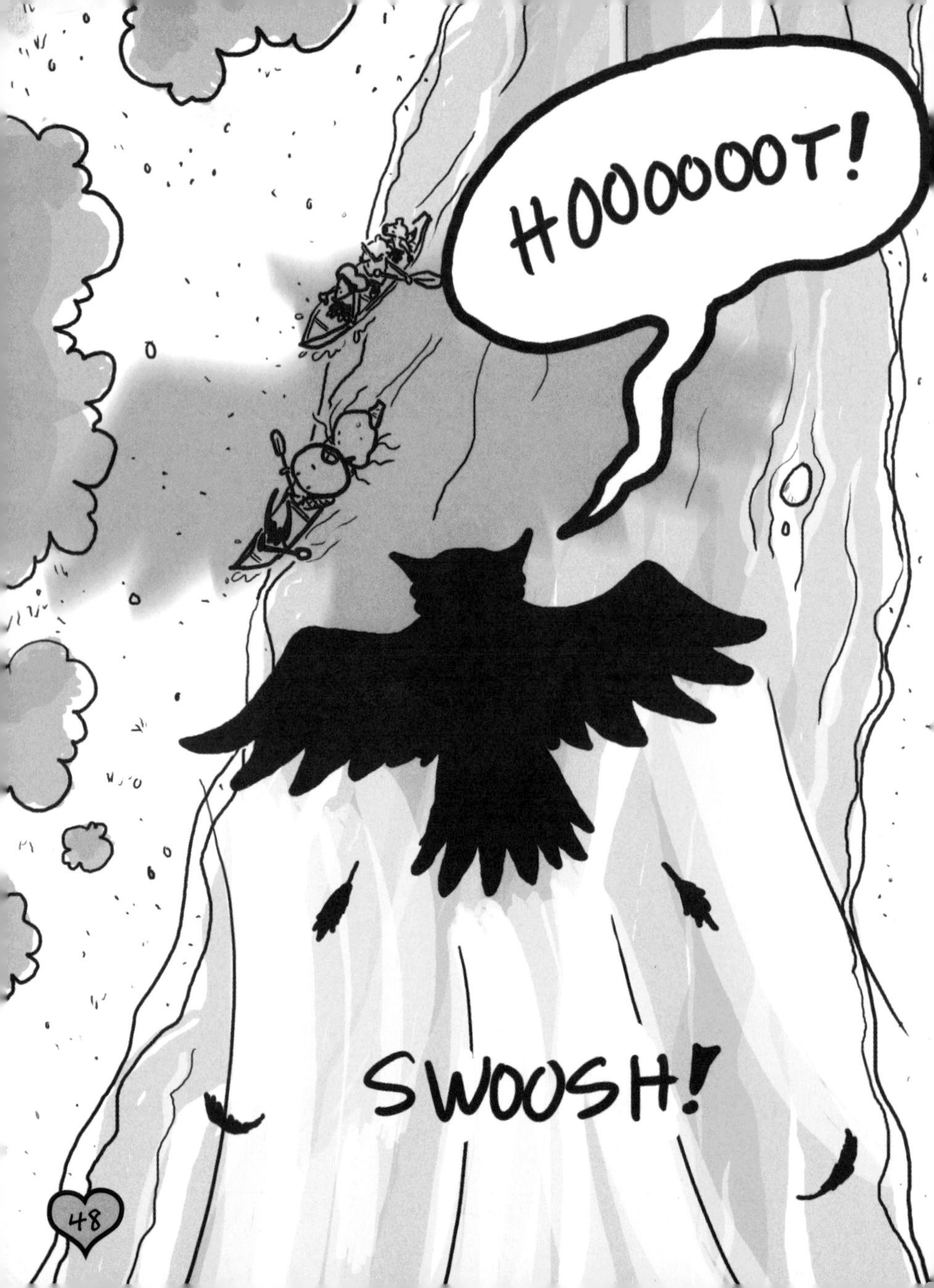
HOOOOOOT!
SWOOSH!

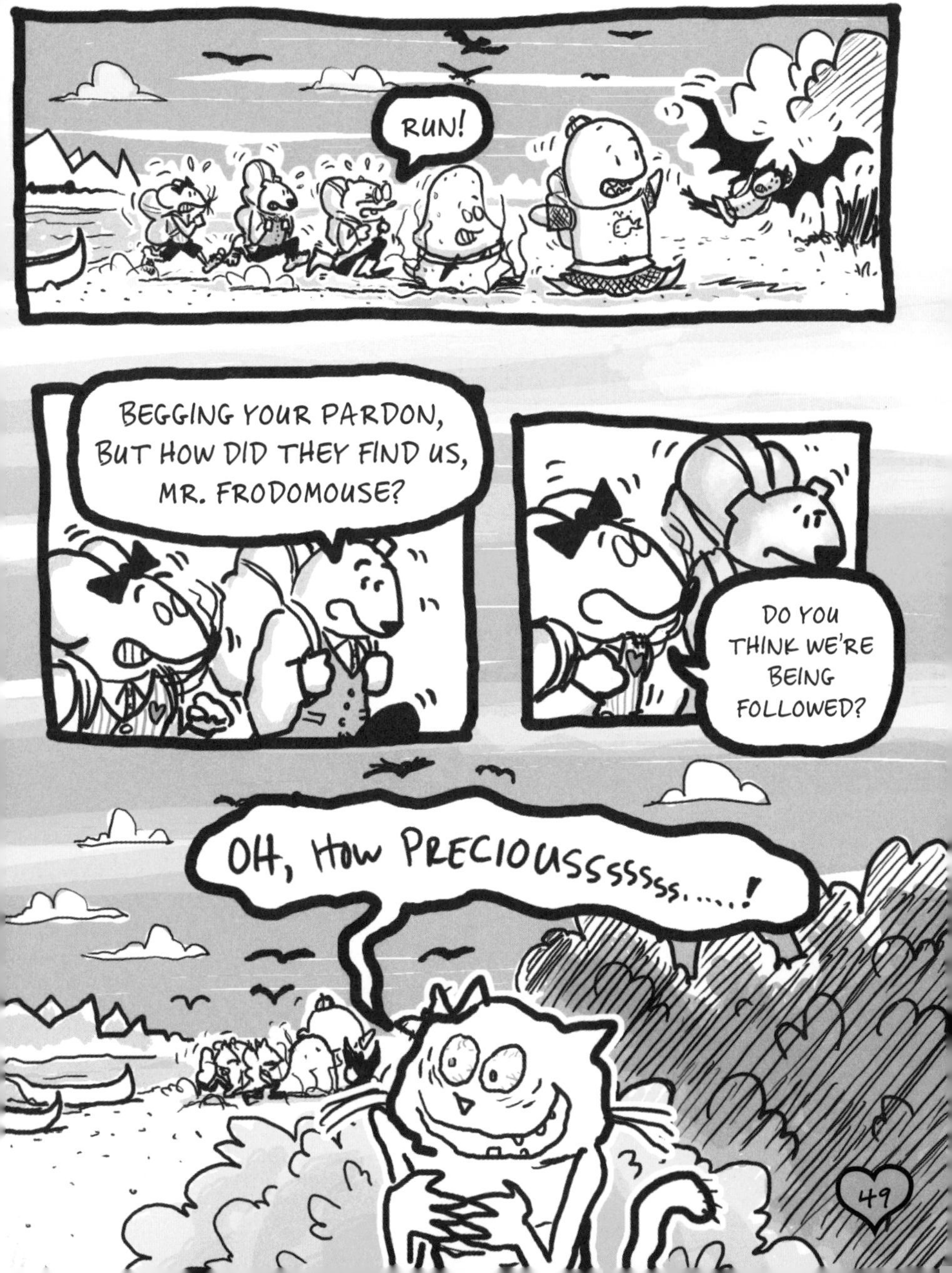
RUN!
BEGGING YOUR PARDON, BUT HOW DID THEY FIND US, MR. FRODOMOUSE?
DO YOU THINK WE'RE BEING FOLLOWED?
OH, HOW PRECIOUSSSSSSSS.....!

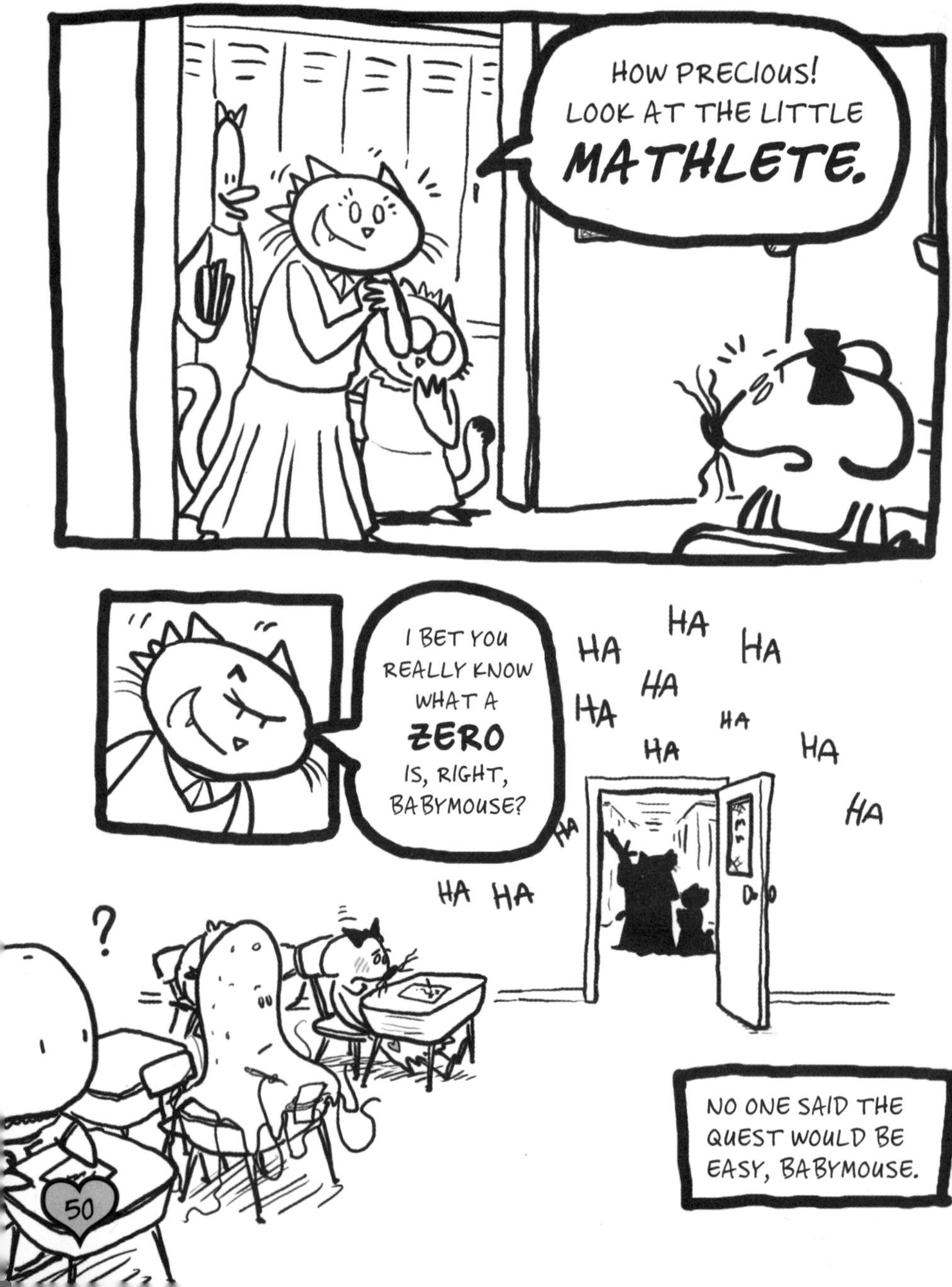
HOW PRECIOUS! LOOK AT THE LITTLE **MATHLETE.**
I BET YOU REALLY KNOW WHAT A **ZERO** IS, RIGHT, BABYMOUSE?
HA HA HA HA HA HA HA HA HA HA HA HA HA
?
NO ONE SAID THE QUEST WOULD BE EASY, BABYMOUSE.

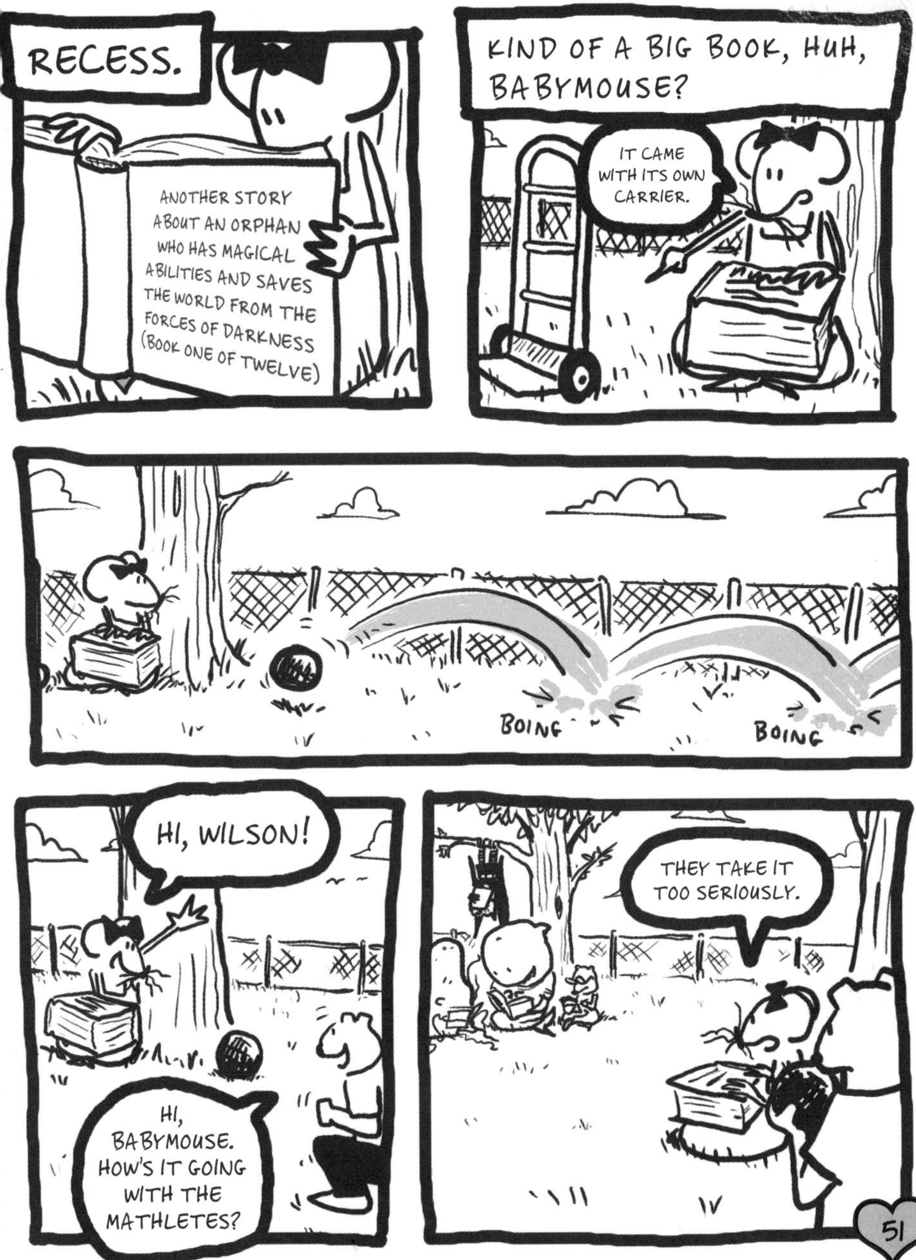
RECESS.
ANOTHER STORY ABOUT AN ORPHAN WHO HAS MAGICAL ABILITIES AND SAVES THE WORLD FROM THE FORCES OF DARKNESS (BOOK ONE OF TWELVE)
KIND OF A BIG BOOK, HUH, BABYMOUSE?
IT CAME WITH ITS OWN CARRIER.
BOING
BOING
HI, WILSON!
HI, BABYMOUSE. HOW'S IT GOING WITH THE MATHLETES?
THEY TAKE IT TOO SERIOUSLY.

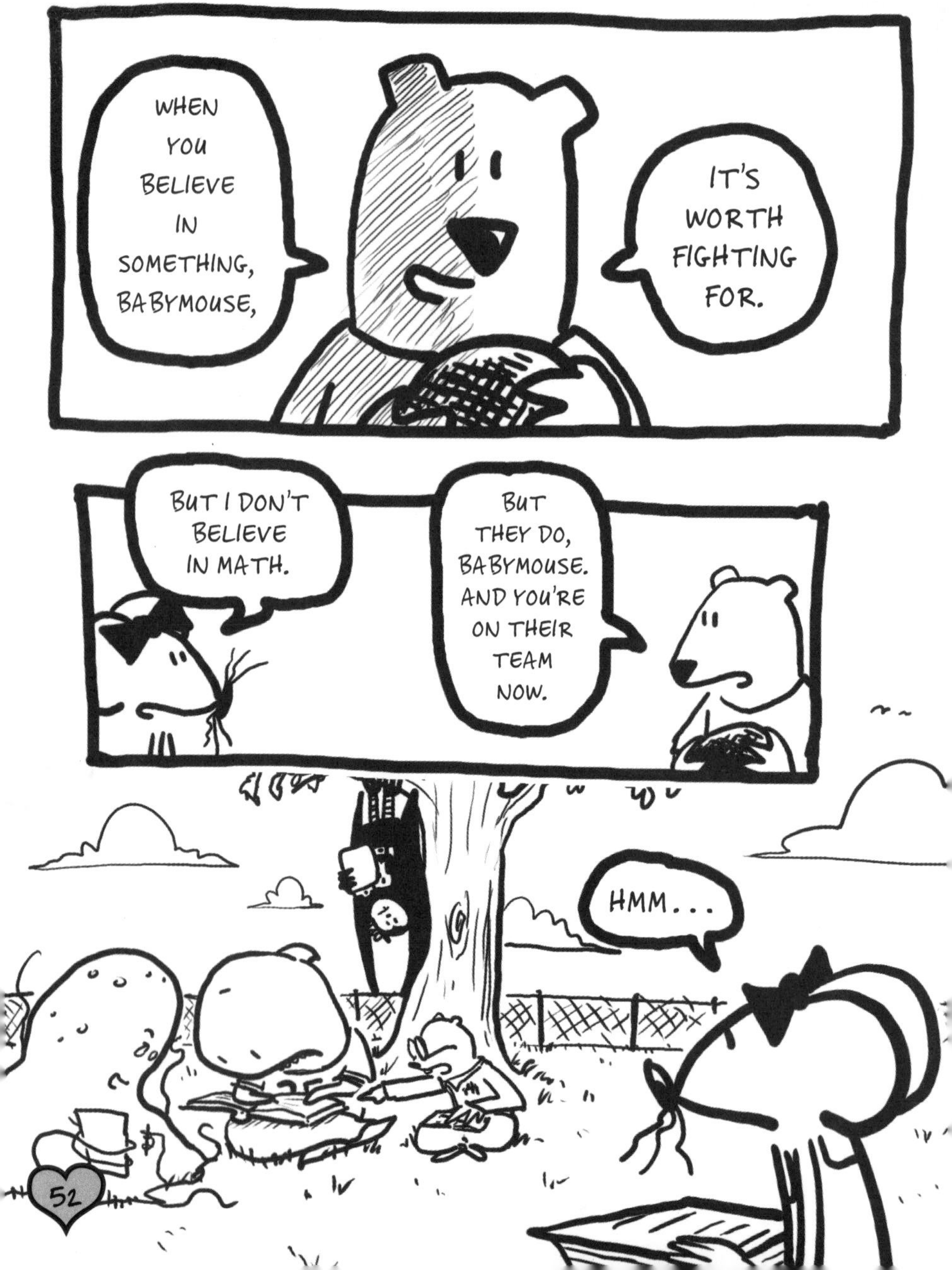
WHEN YOU BELIEVE IN SOMETHING, BABYMOUSE,
IT'S WORTH FIGHTING FOR.
BUT I DON'T BELIEVE IN MATH.
BUT THEY DO, BABYMOUSE. AND YOU'RE ON THEIR TEAM NOW.
HMM...

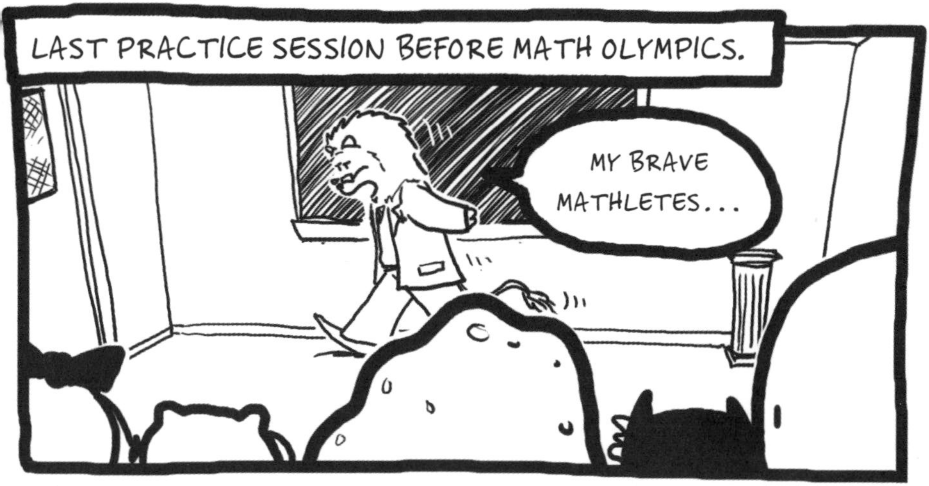
LAST PRACTICE SESSION BEFORE MATH OLYMPICS.
MY BRAVE MATHLETES...

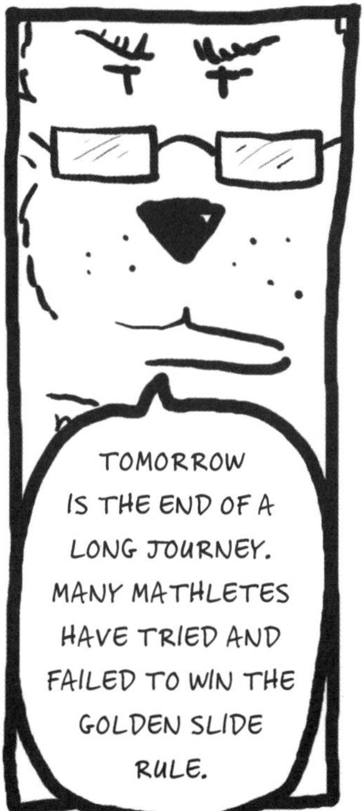
TOMORROW IS THE END OF A LONG JOURNEY. MANY MATHLETES HAVE TRIED AND FAILED TO WIN THE GOLDEN SLIDE RULE.

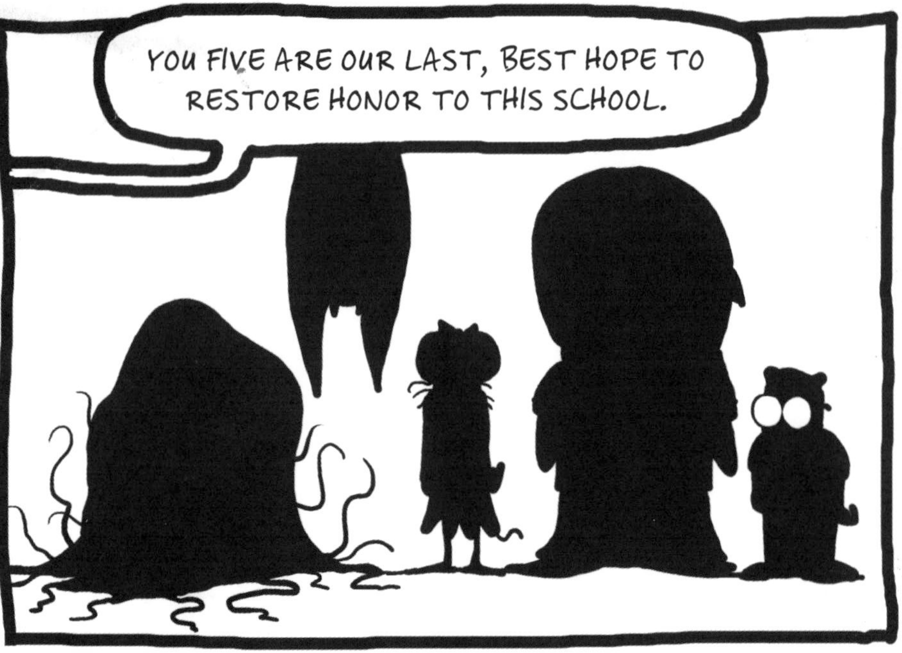
YOU FIVE ARE OUR LAST, BEST HOPE TO RESTORE HONOR TO THIS SCHOOL.

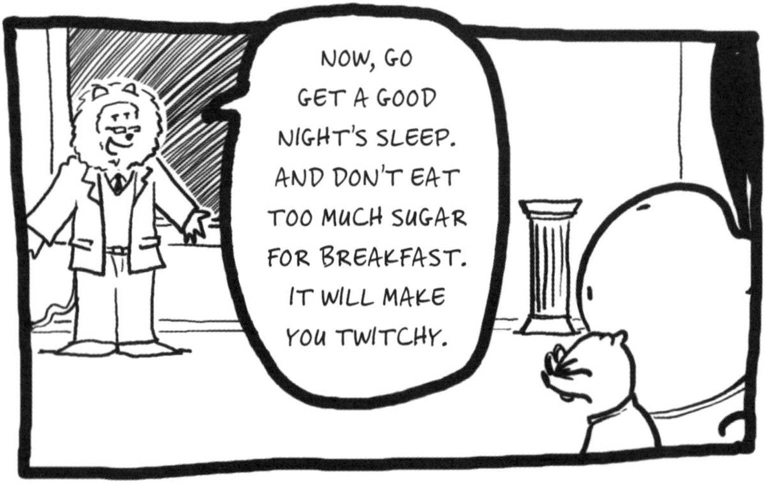
NOW, GO GET A GOOD NIGHT'S SLEEP. AND DON'T EAT TOO MUCH SUGAR FOR BREAKFAST. IT WILL MAKE YOU TWITCHY.

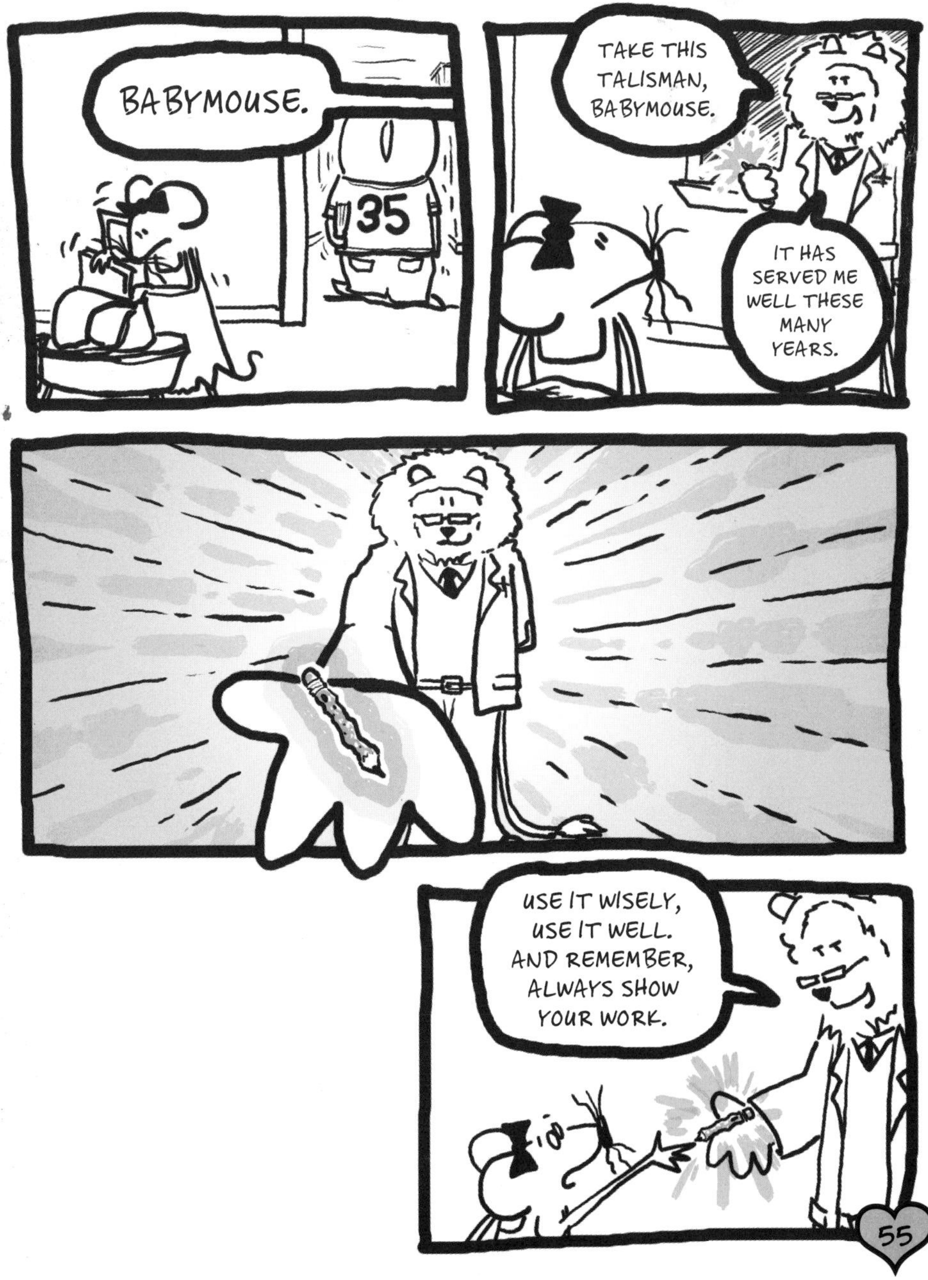
BABYMOUSE.
TAKE THIS TALISMAN, BABYMOUSE.
IT HAS SERVED ME WELL THESE MANY YEARS.
USE IT WISELY, USE IT WELL. AND REMEMBER, ALWAYS SHOW YOUR WORK.

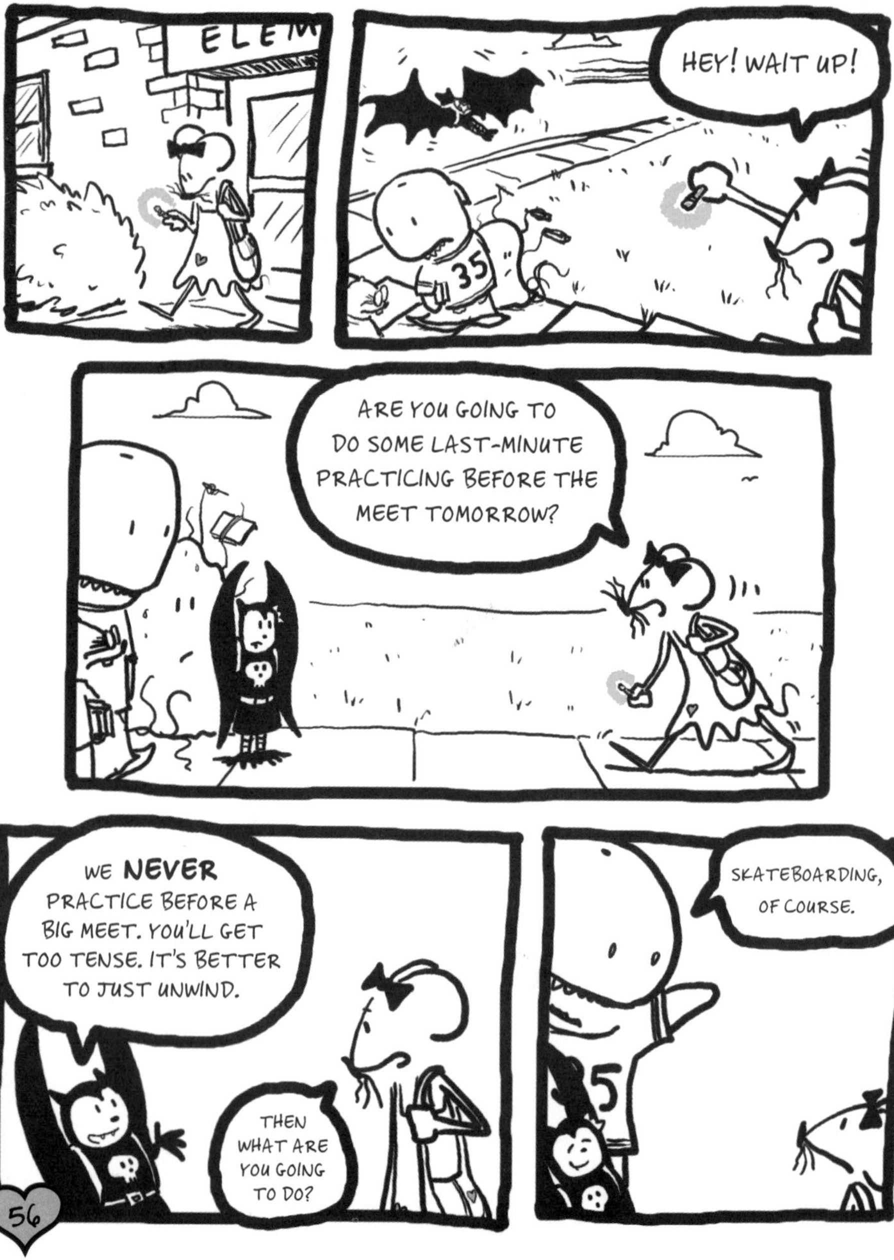
ELEM
HEY! WAIT UP!
ARE YOU GOING TO DO SOME LAST-MINUTE PRACTICING BEFORE THE MEET TOMORROW?
WE NEVER PRACTICE BEFORE A BIG MEET. YOU'LL GET TOO TENSE. IT'S BETTER TO JUST UNWIND.
THEN WHAT ARE YOU GOING TO DO?
SKATEBOARDING, OF COURSE.

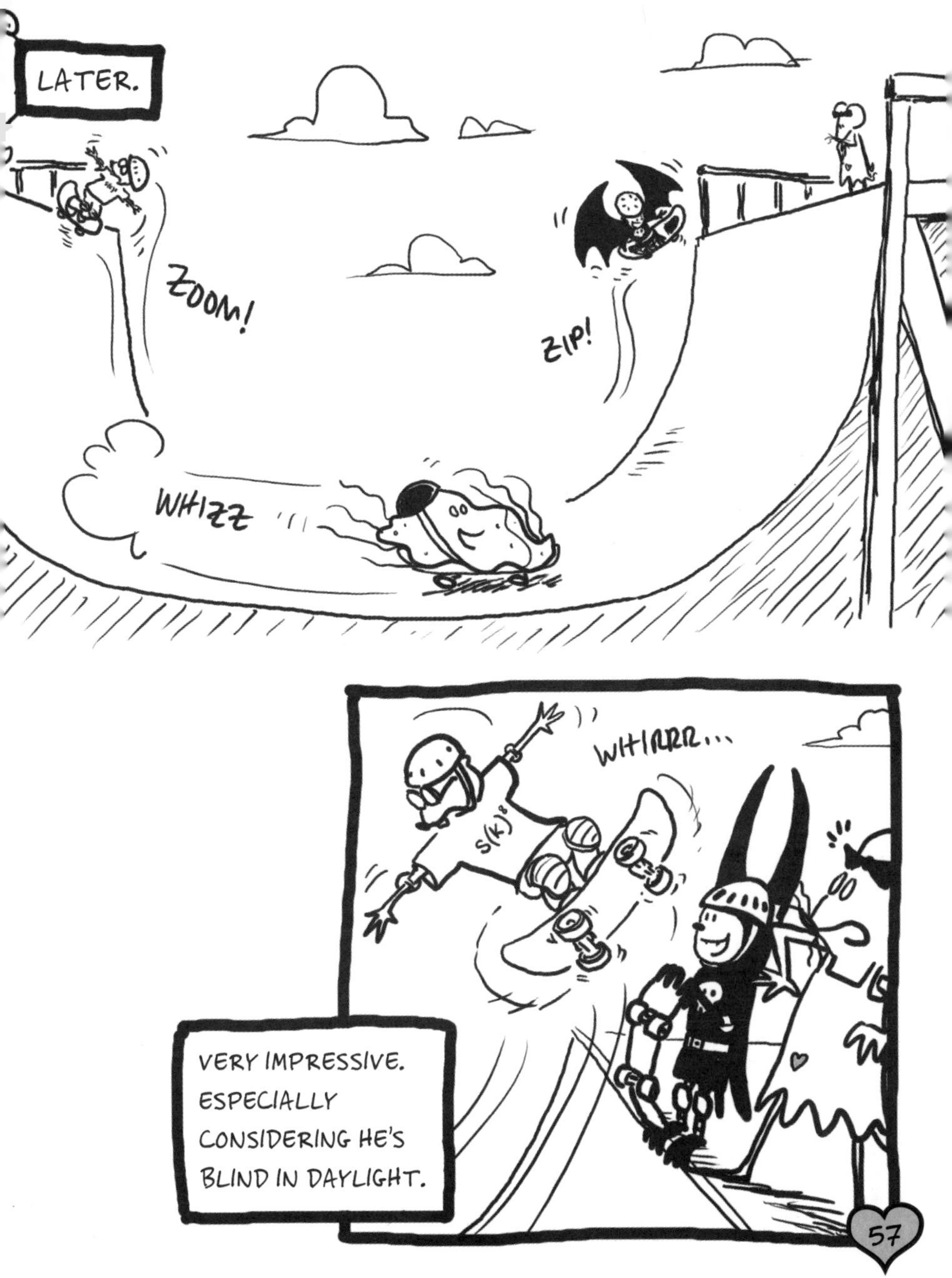
LATER.
ZOOM!
ZIP!
WHIZZ
WHIRRR...
S(K)8
VERY IMPRESSIVE. ESPECIALLY CONSIDERING HE'S BLIND IN DAYLIGHT.

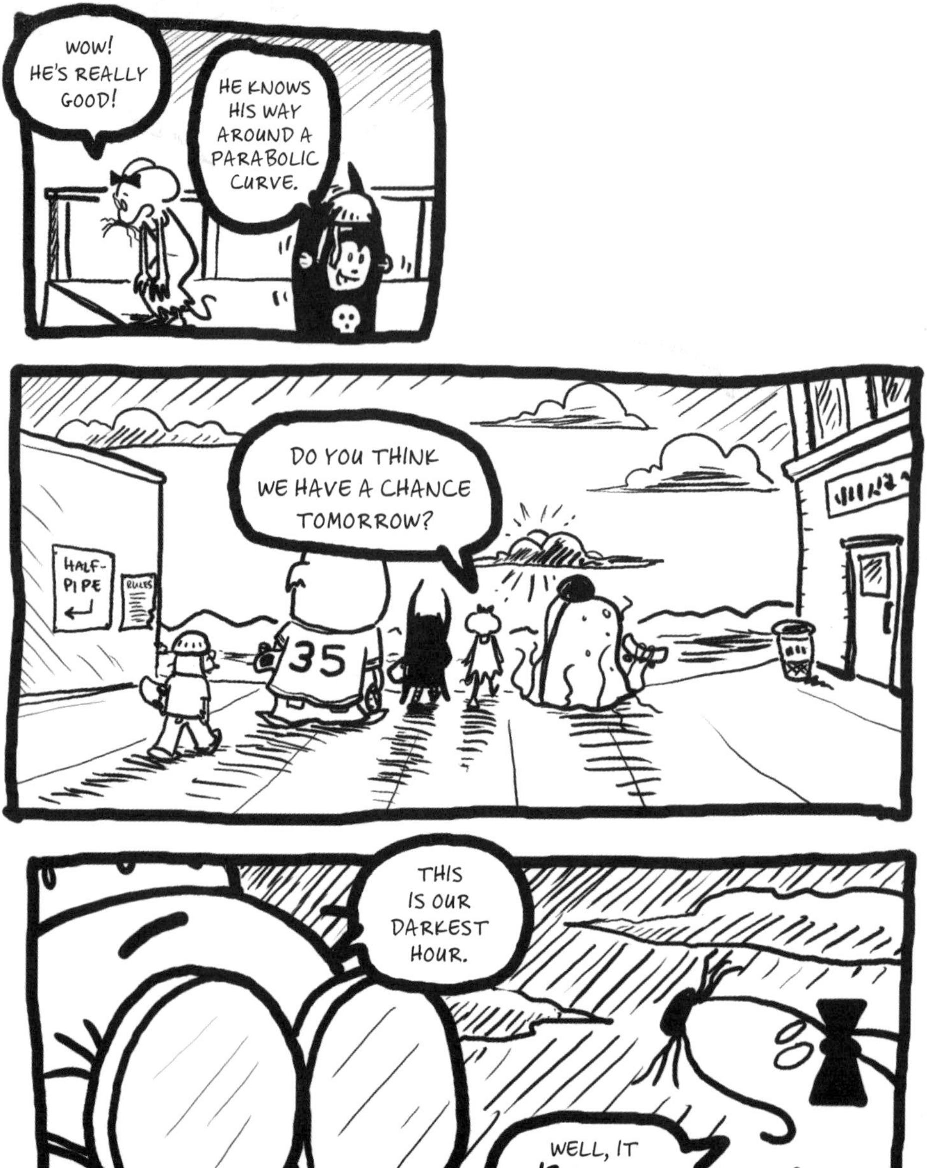
WOW! HE'S REALLY GOOD!
HE KNOWS HIS WAY AROUND A PARABOLIC CURVE.
DO YOU THINK WE HAVE A CHANCE TOMORROW?
HALF-PIPE
RULES
THIS IS OUR DARKEST HOUR.
WELL, IT **IS** ALMOST DINNERTIME.

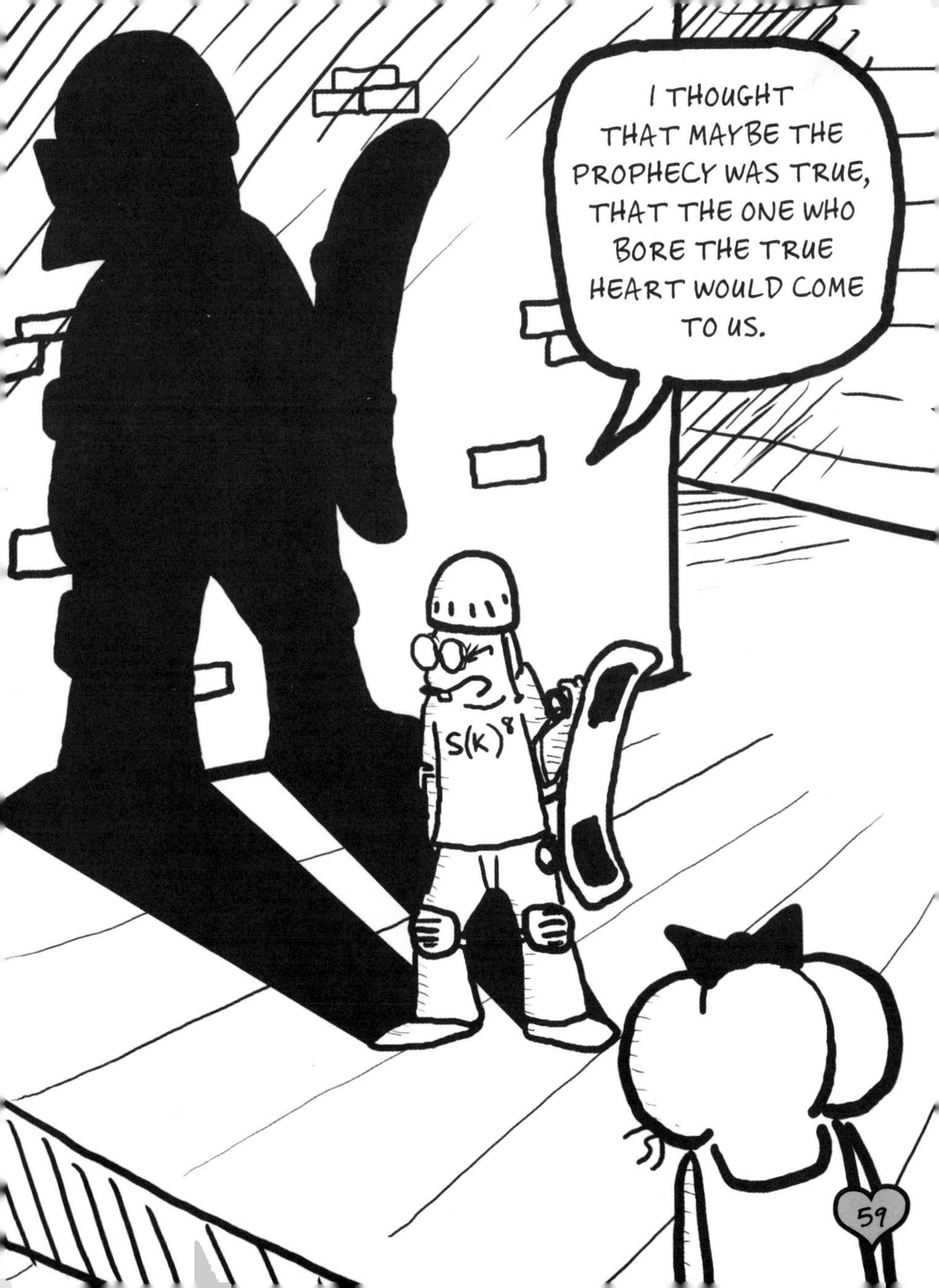
I THOUGHT THAT MAYBE THE PROPHECY WAS TRUE, THAT THE ONE WHO BORE THE TRUE HEART WOULD COME TO US.
S(K)8

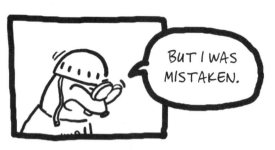

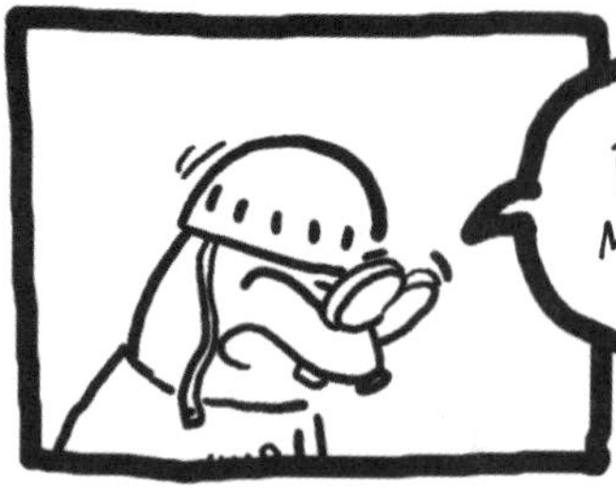
BUT I WAS MISTAKEN.

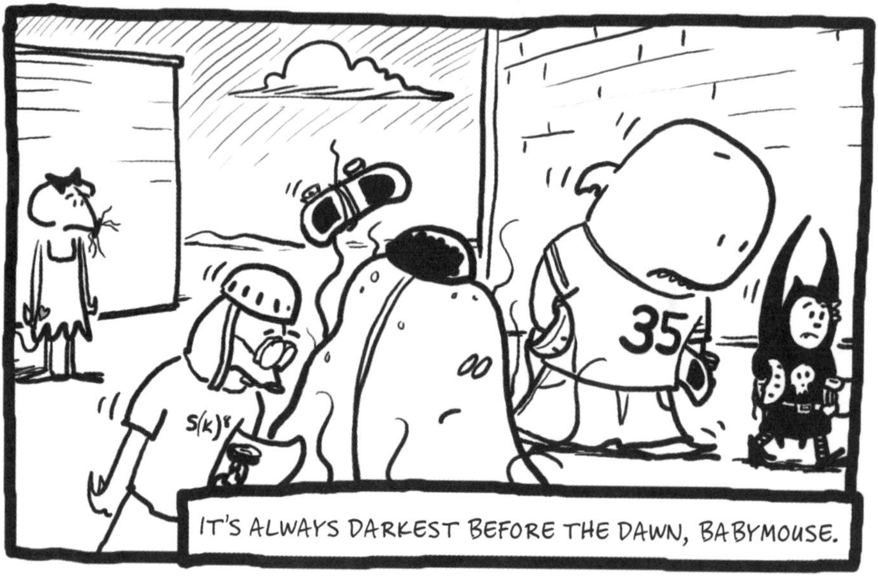
35
IT'S ALWAYS DARKEST BEFORE THE DAWN, BABYMOUSE.

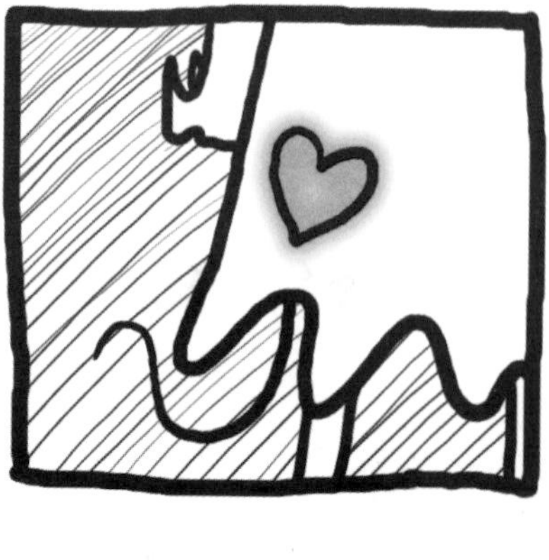

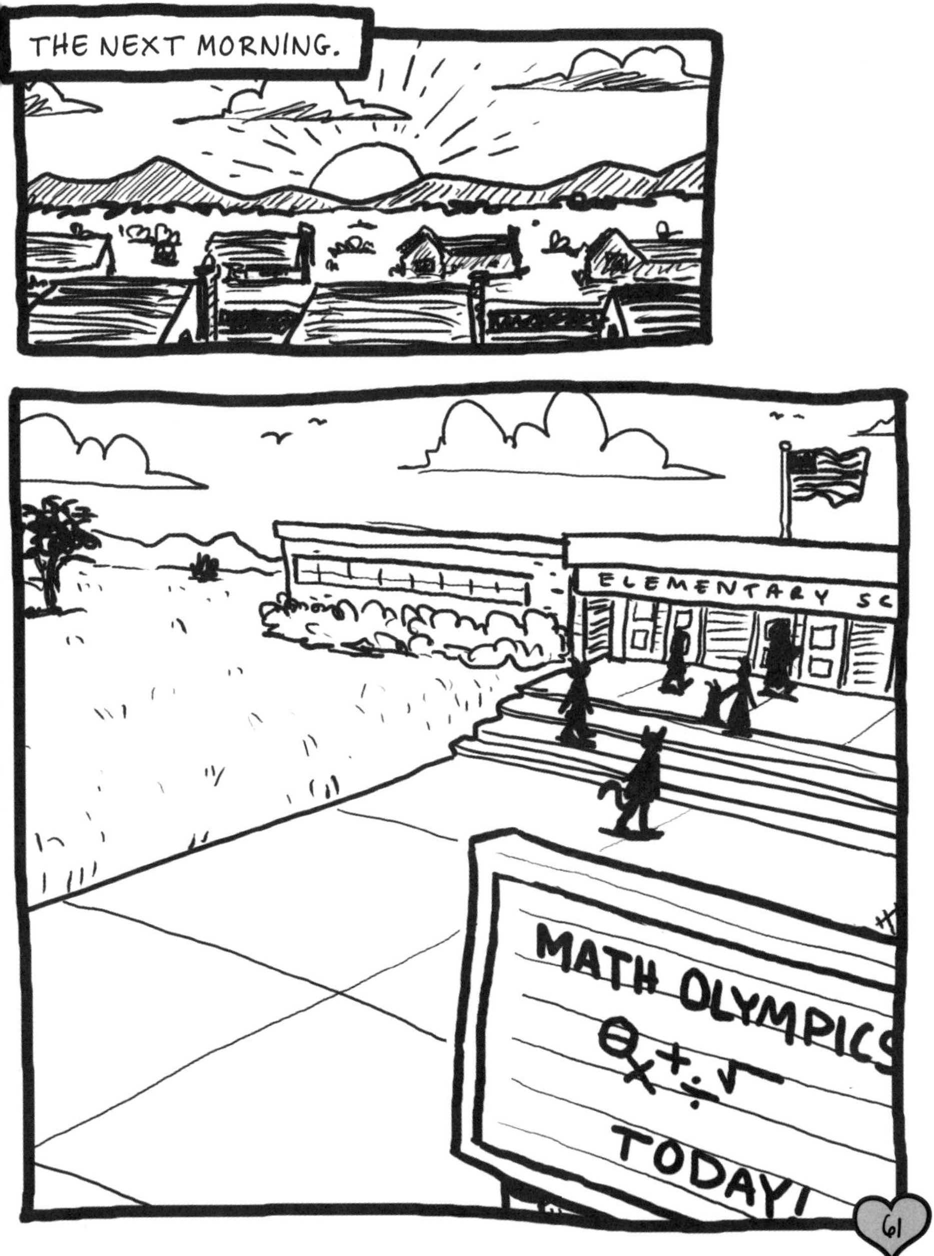
THE NEXT MORNING.
ELEMENTARY SC
MATH OLYMPICS
TODAY!

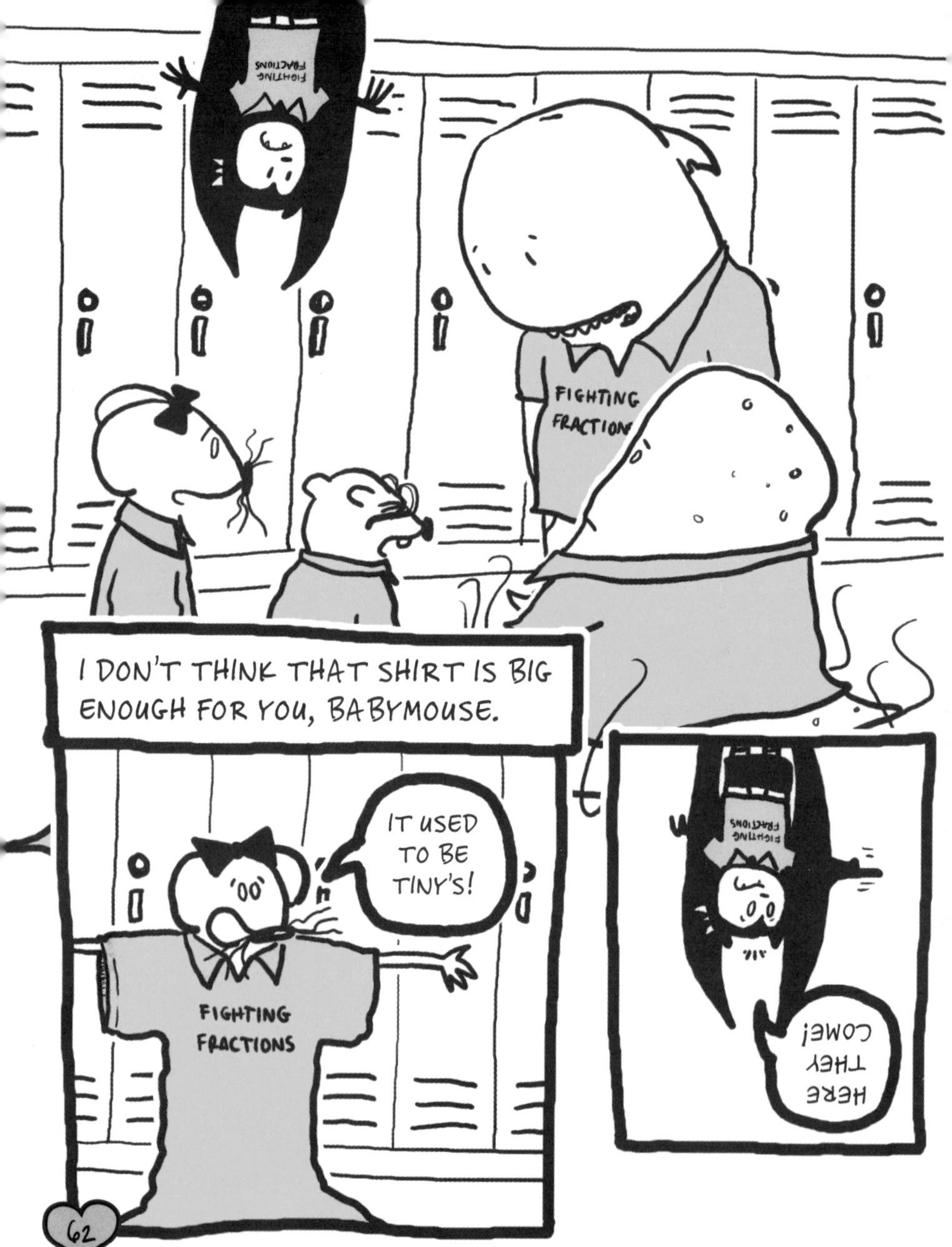
FIGHTING FRACTIONS
I DON'T THINK THAT SHIRT IS BIG ENOUGH FOR YOU, BABYMOUSE.
IT USED TO BE TINY'S!
FIGHTING FRACTIONS
HERE THEY COME!

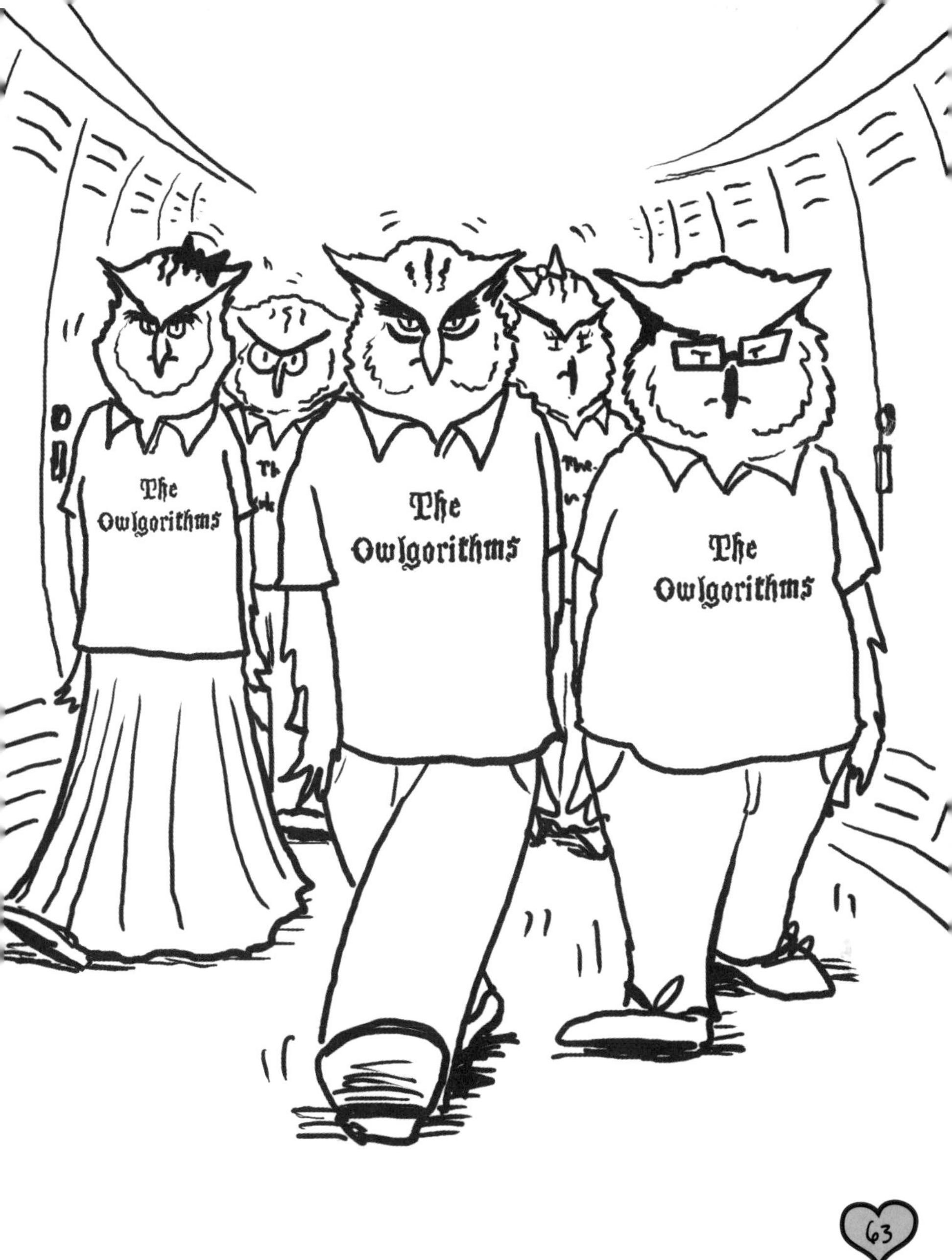
The Owlgorithms
The Owlgorithms
The Owlgorithms

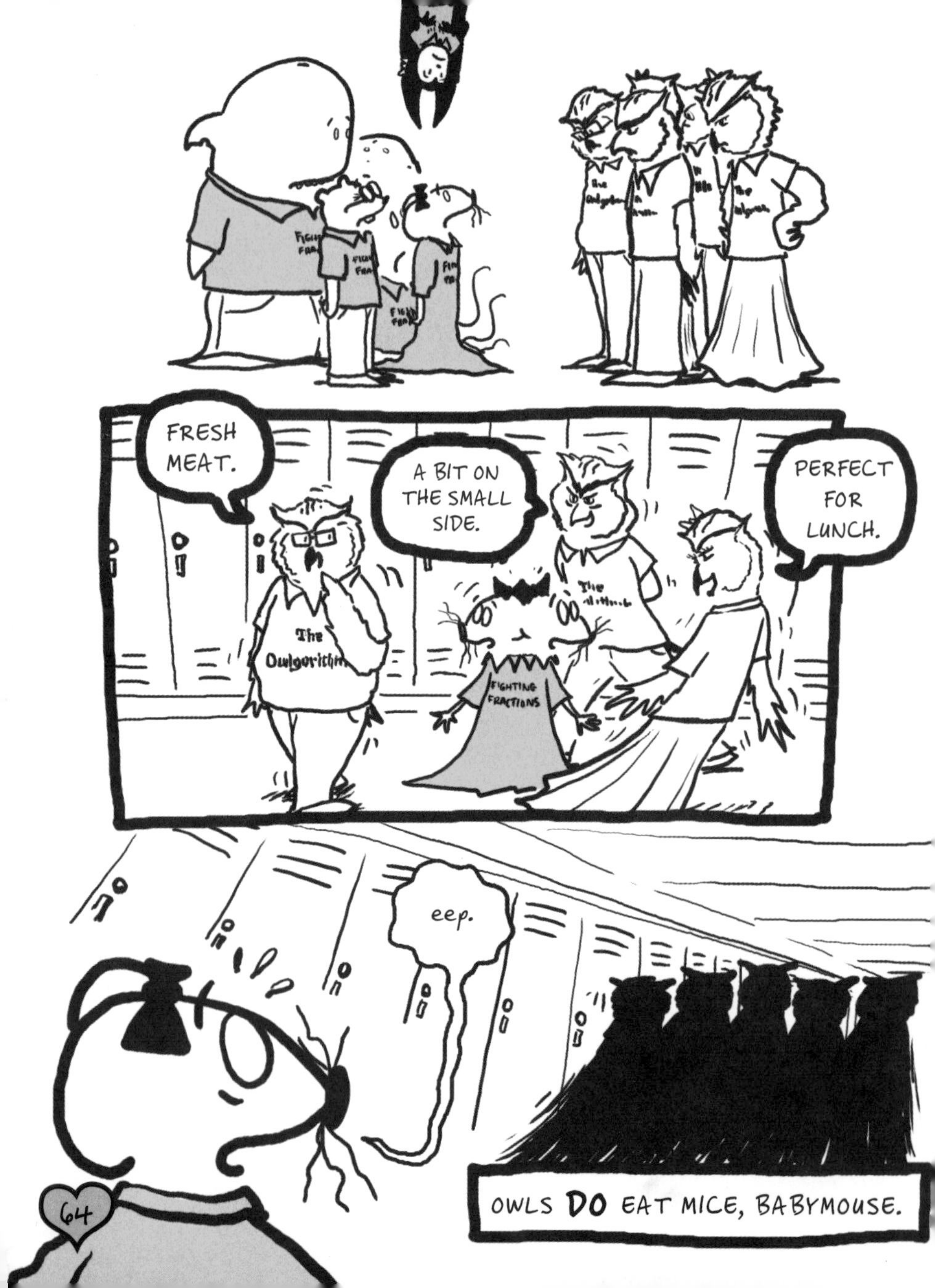

FRESH MEAT.
A BIT ON THE SMALL SIDE.
PERFECT FOR LUNCH.
eep.
OWLS DO EAT MICE, BABYMOUSE.

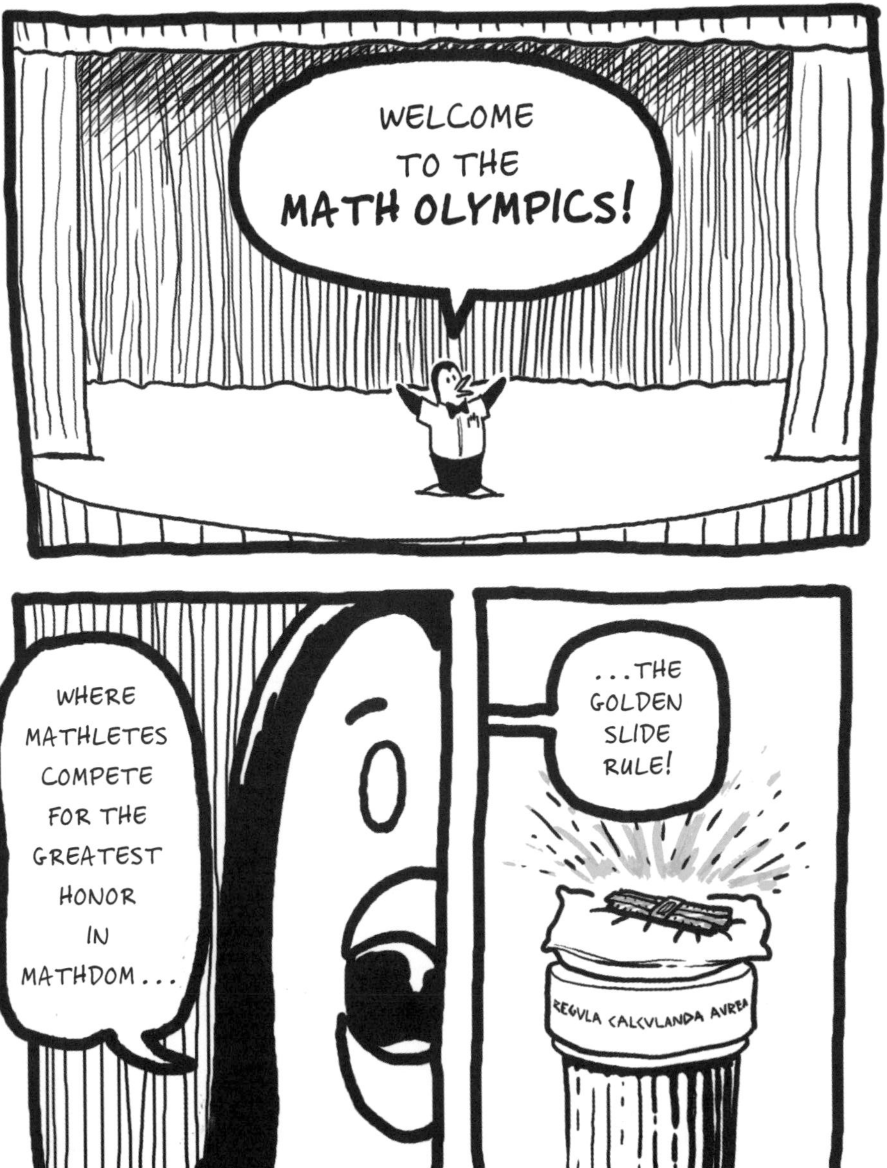
WELCOME TO THE MATH OLYMPICS!
WHERE MATHLETES COMPETE FOR THE GREATEST HONOR IN MATHDOM...
...THE GOLDEN SLIDE RULE!
REGVLA CALCVLANDA AVREA

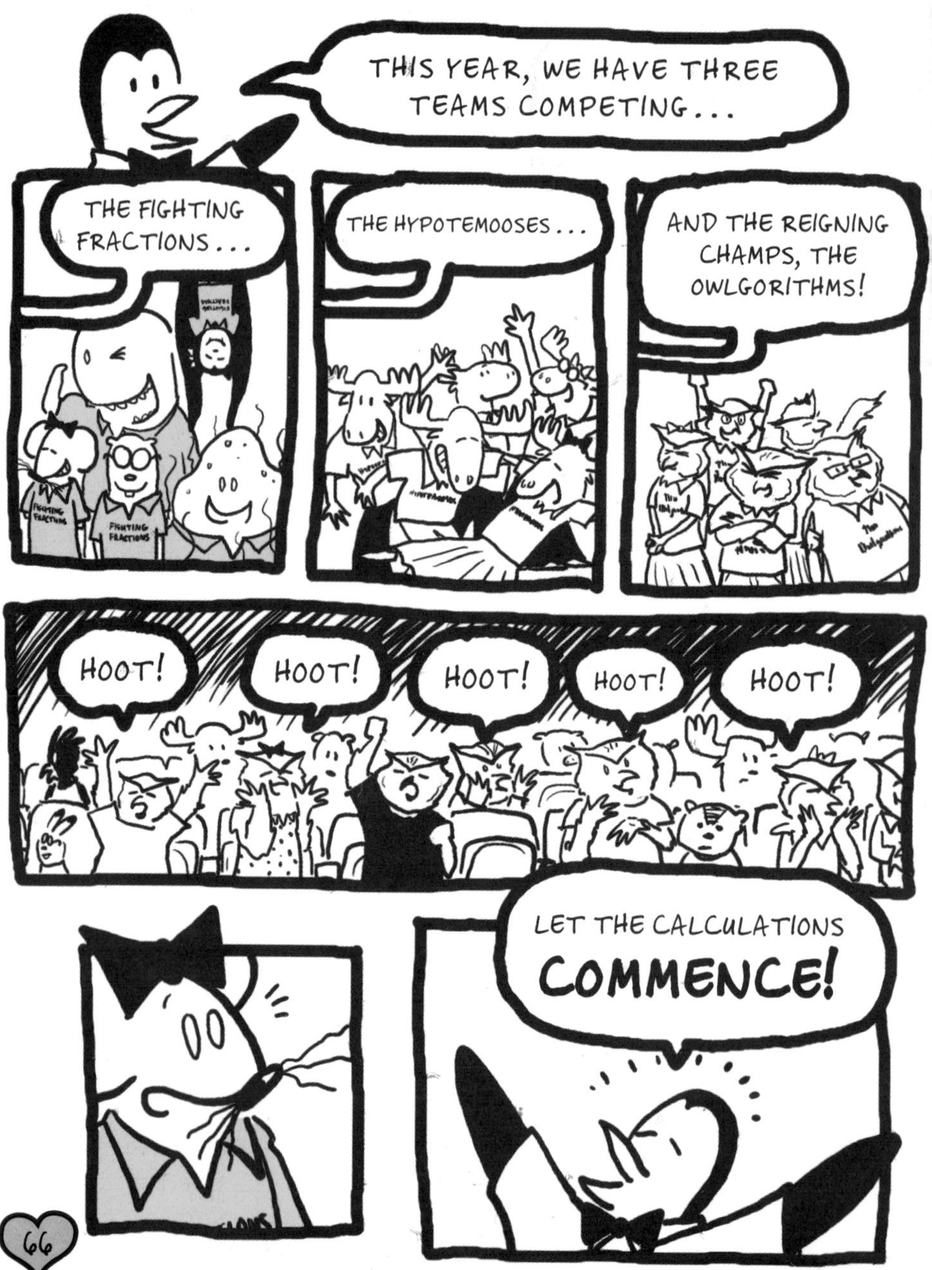
THIS YEAR, WE HAVE THREE TEAMS COMPETING...
THE FIGHTING FRACTIONS...
THE HYPOTEMOOSES...
AND THE REIGNING CHAMPS, THE OWLGORITHMS!
HOOT!
HOOT!
HOOT!
HOOT!
HOOT!
LET THE CALCULATIONS COMMENCE!

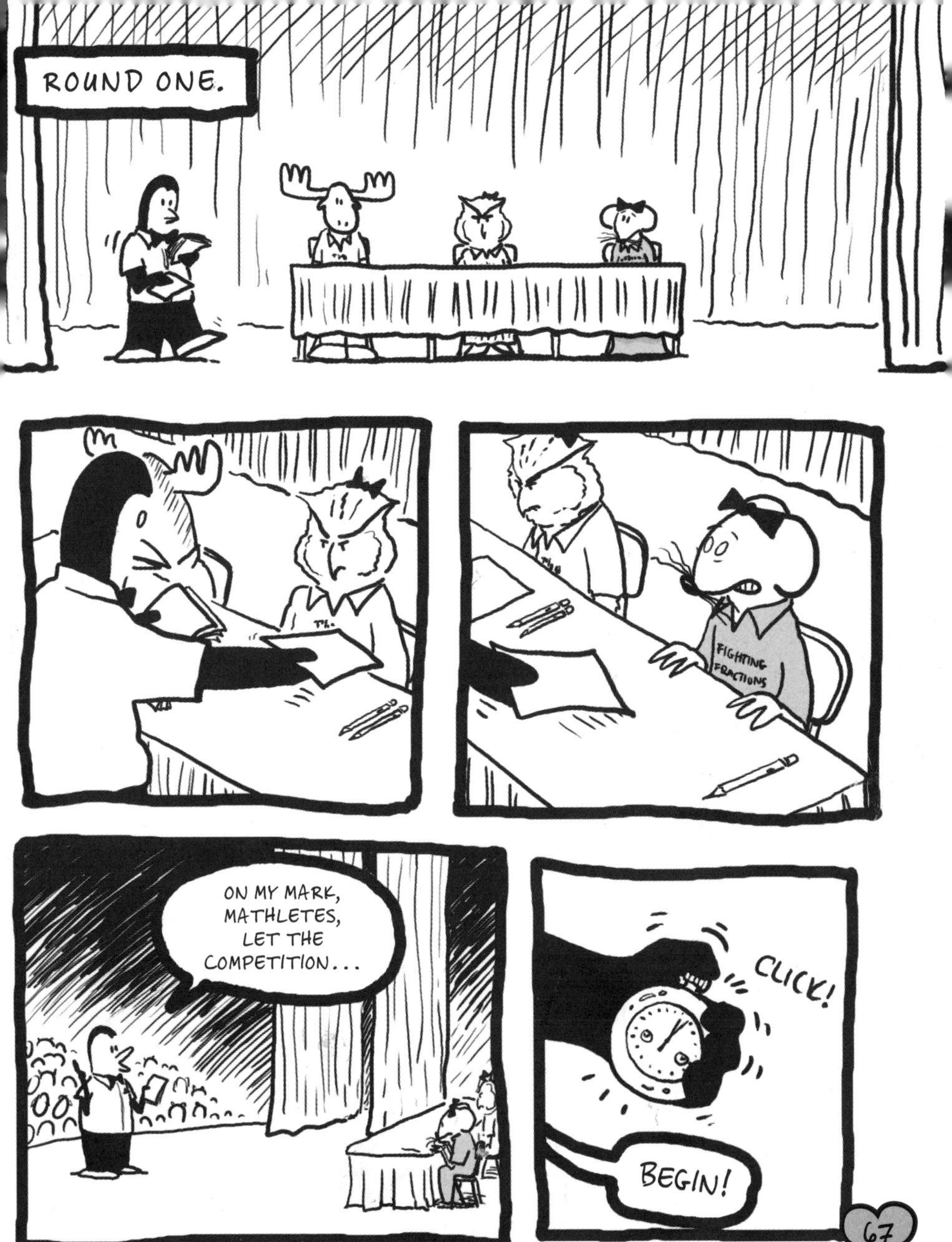
ROUND ONE.
FIGHTING FRACTIONS
ON MY MARK, MATHLETES, LET THE COMPETITION...
CLICK!
BEGIN!

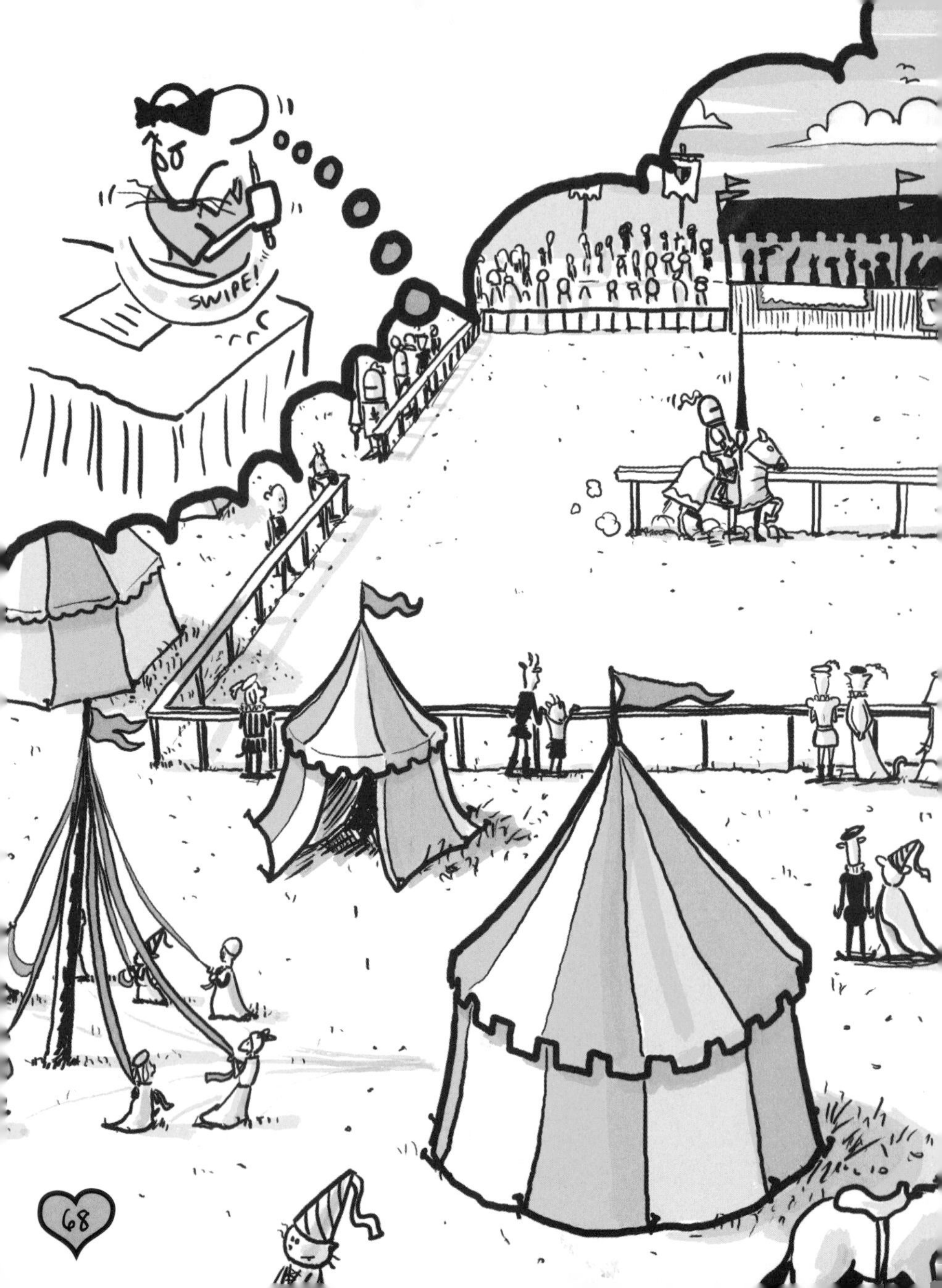
SWIPE!

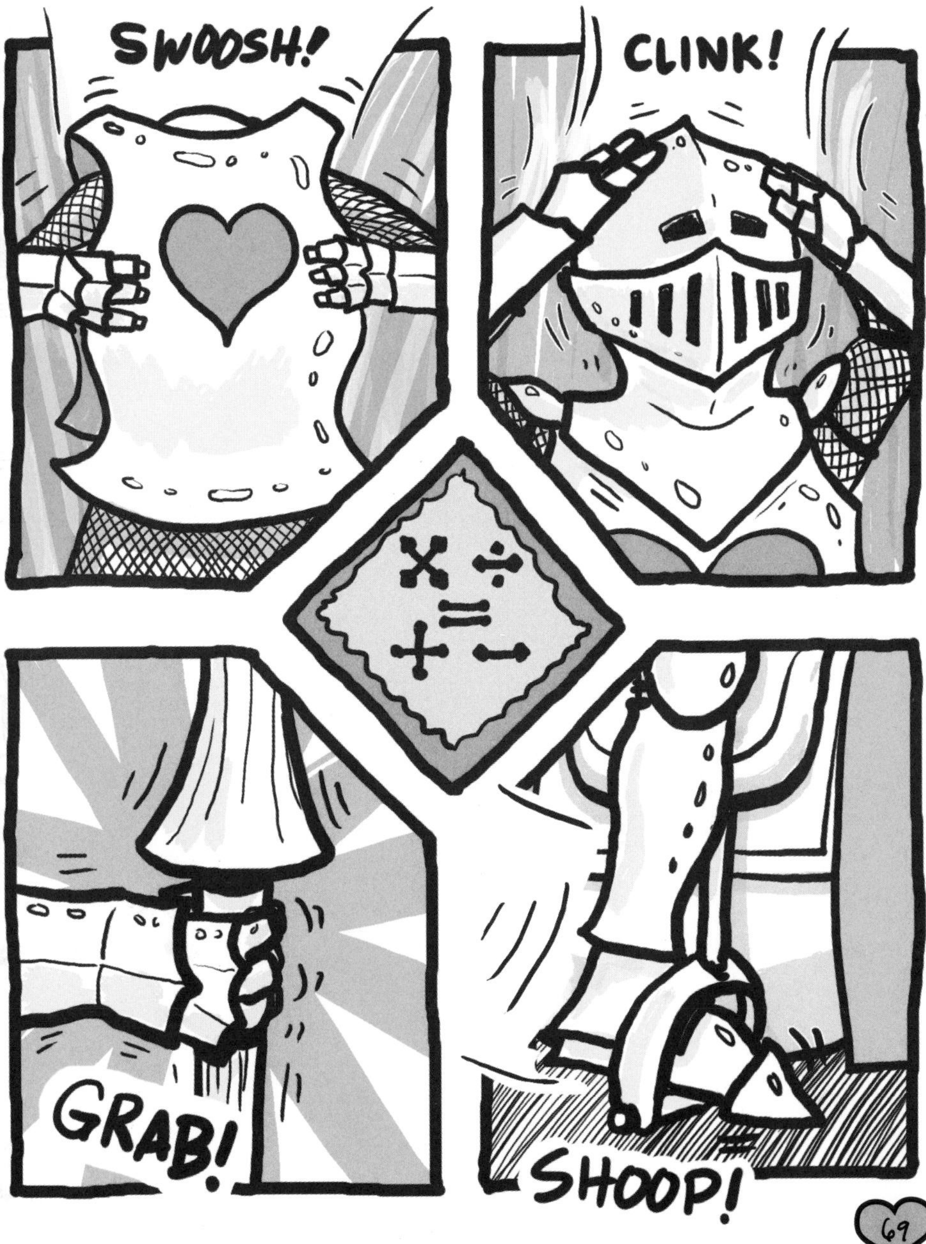
SWOOSH!
CLINK!
× ÷
=
+ −
GRAB!
SHOOP!

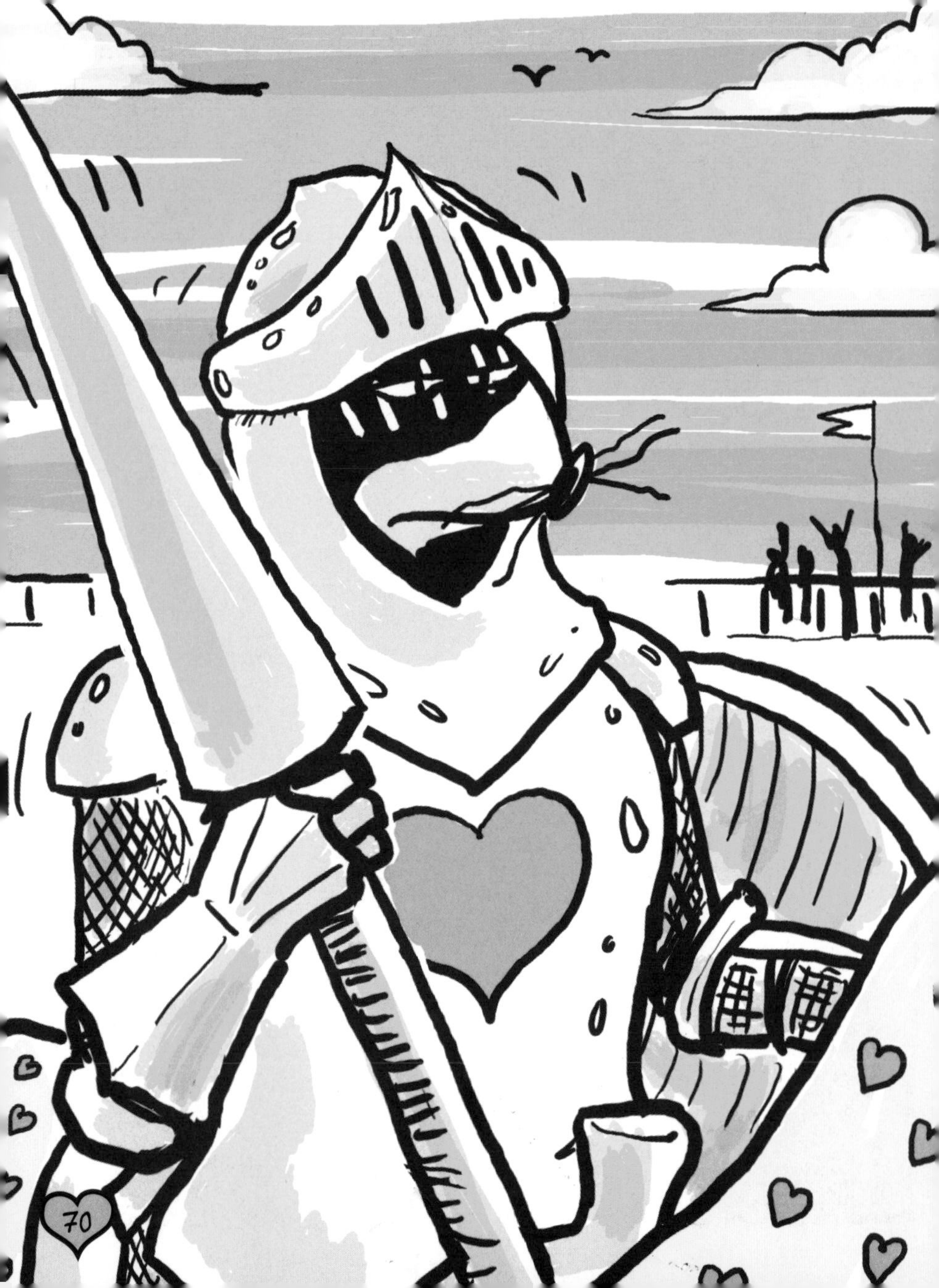

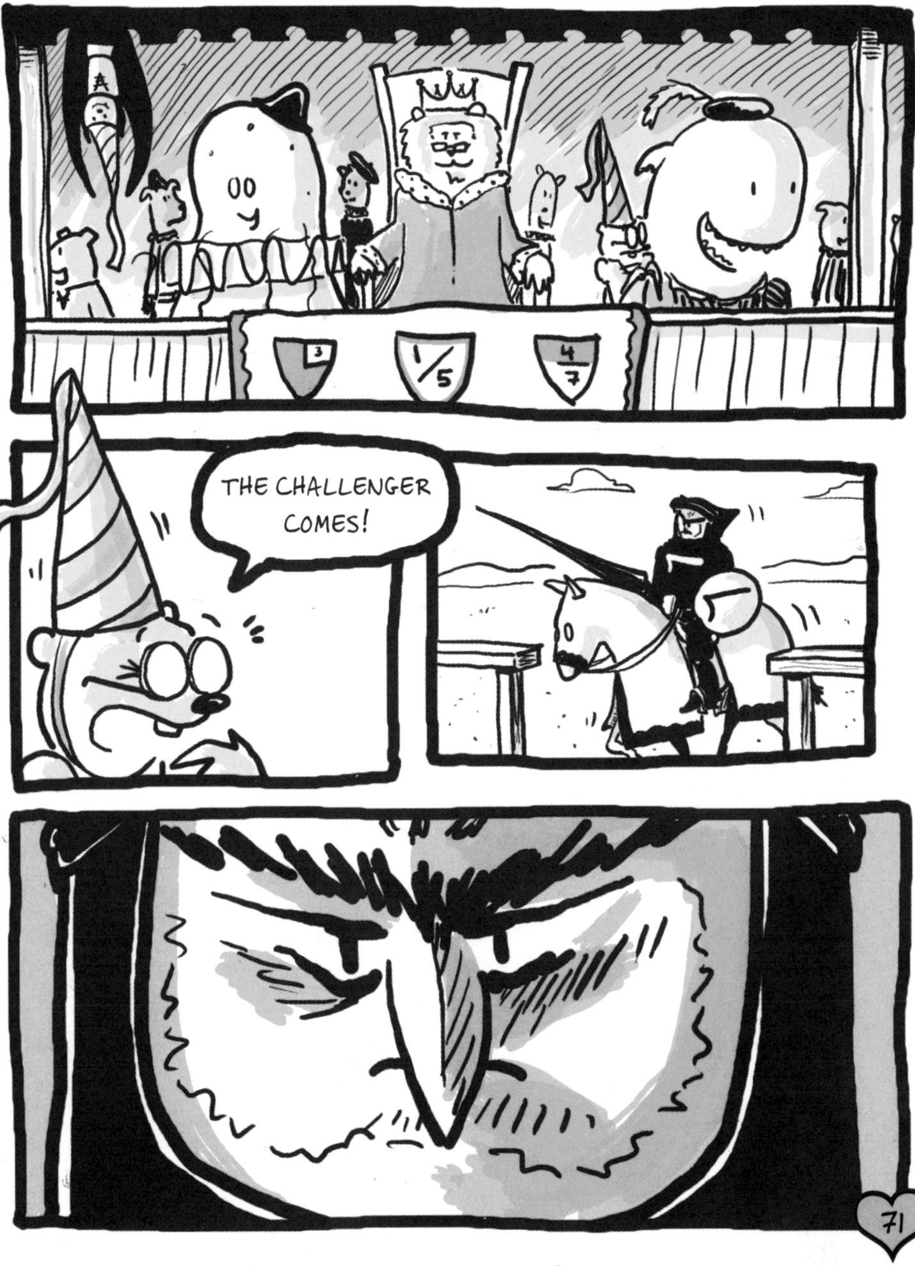
3
1/5
4/7
THE CHALLENGER COMES!

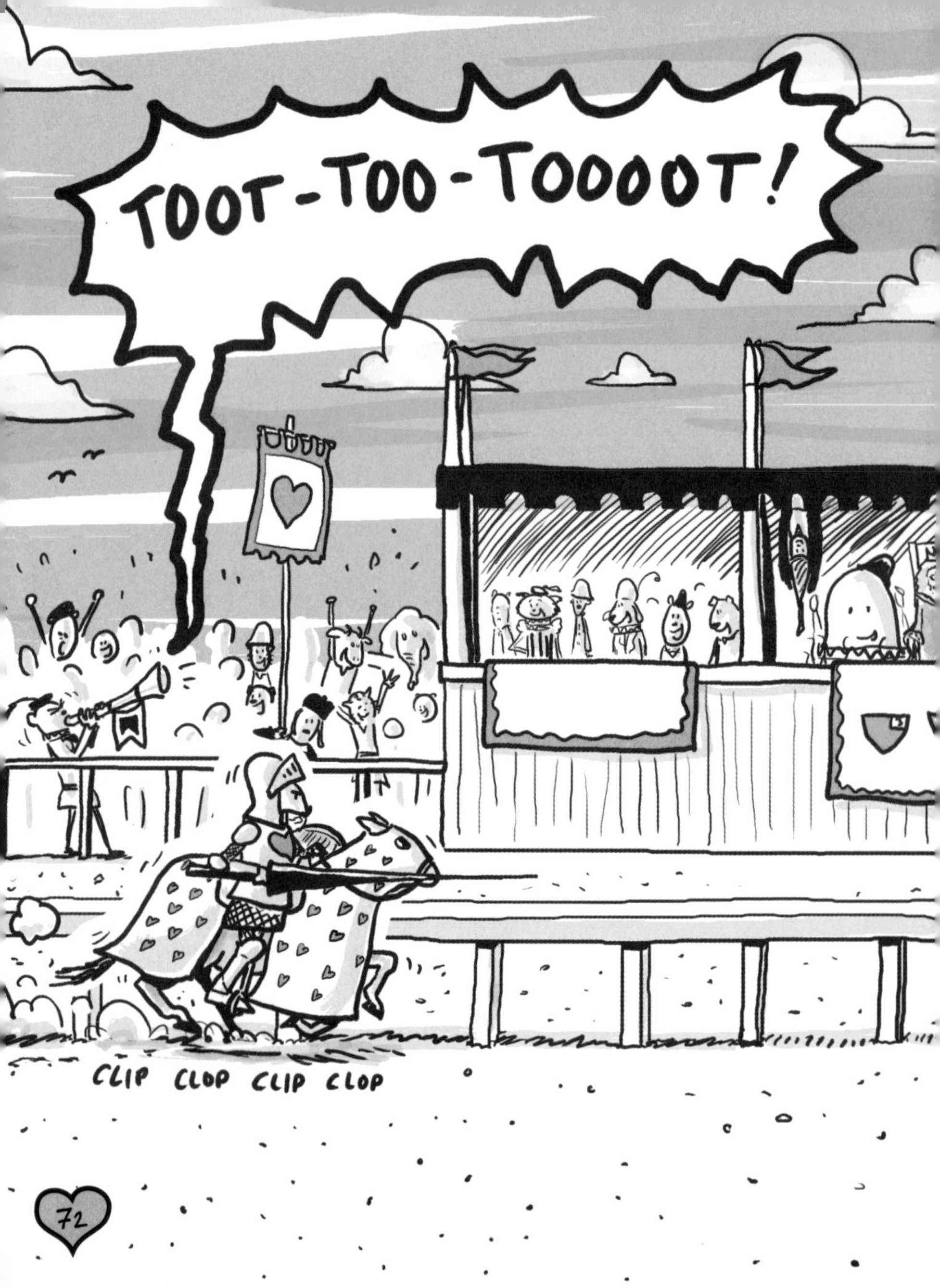
TOOT-TOO-TOOOOT!
CLIP CLOP CLIP CLOP

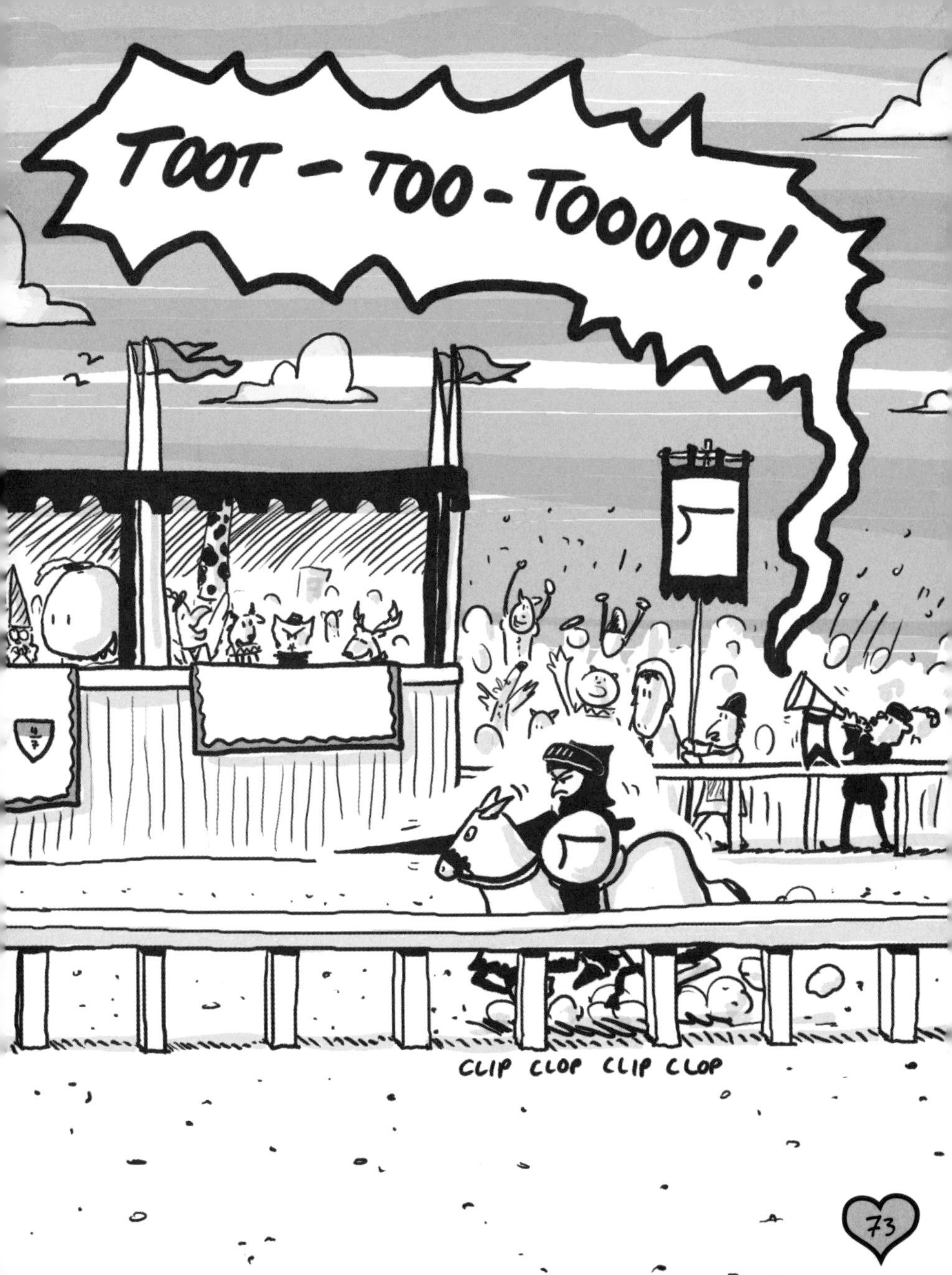
TOOT - TOO - TOOOOT!
CLIP CLOP CLIP CLOP

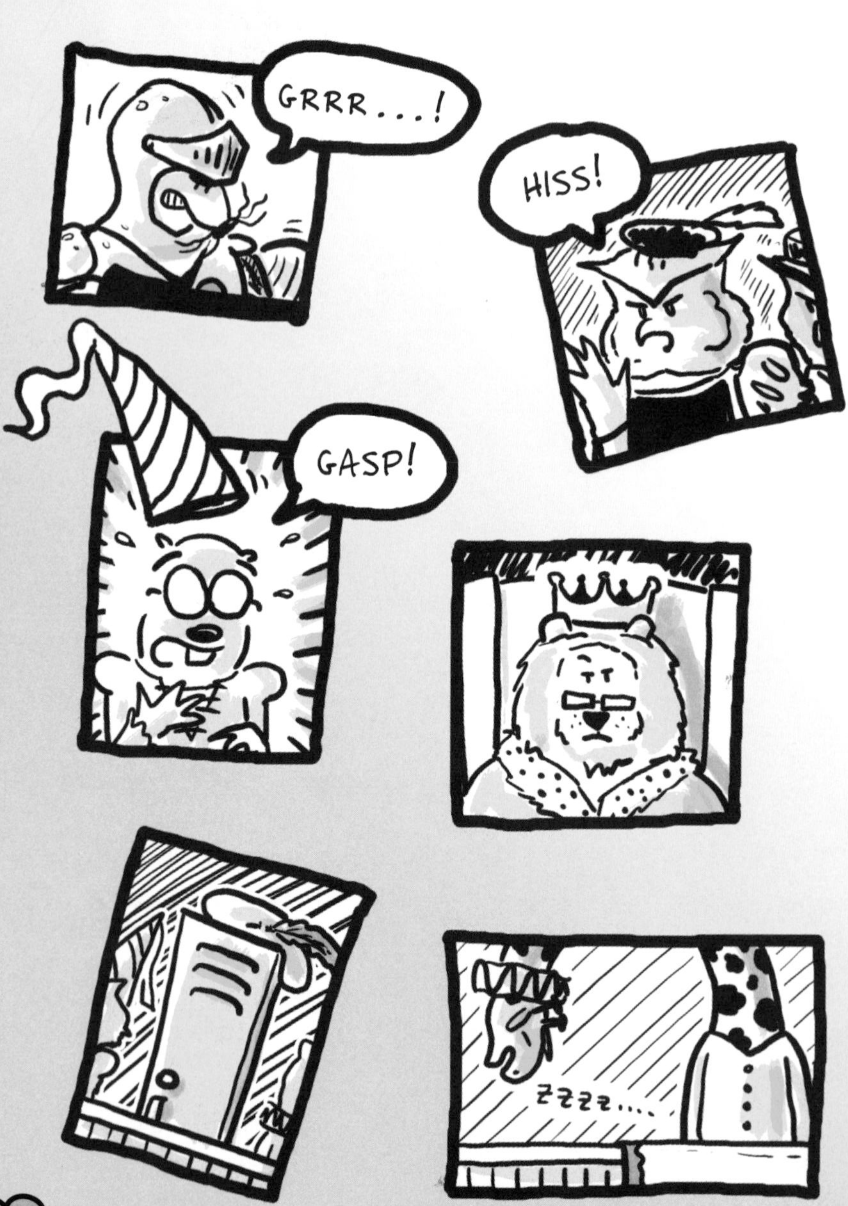
GRRR...!
HISS!
GASP!
ZZZZ....

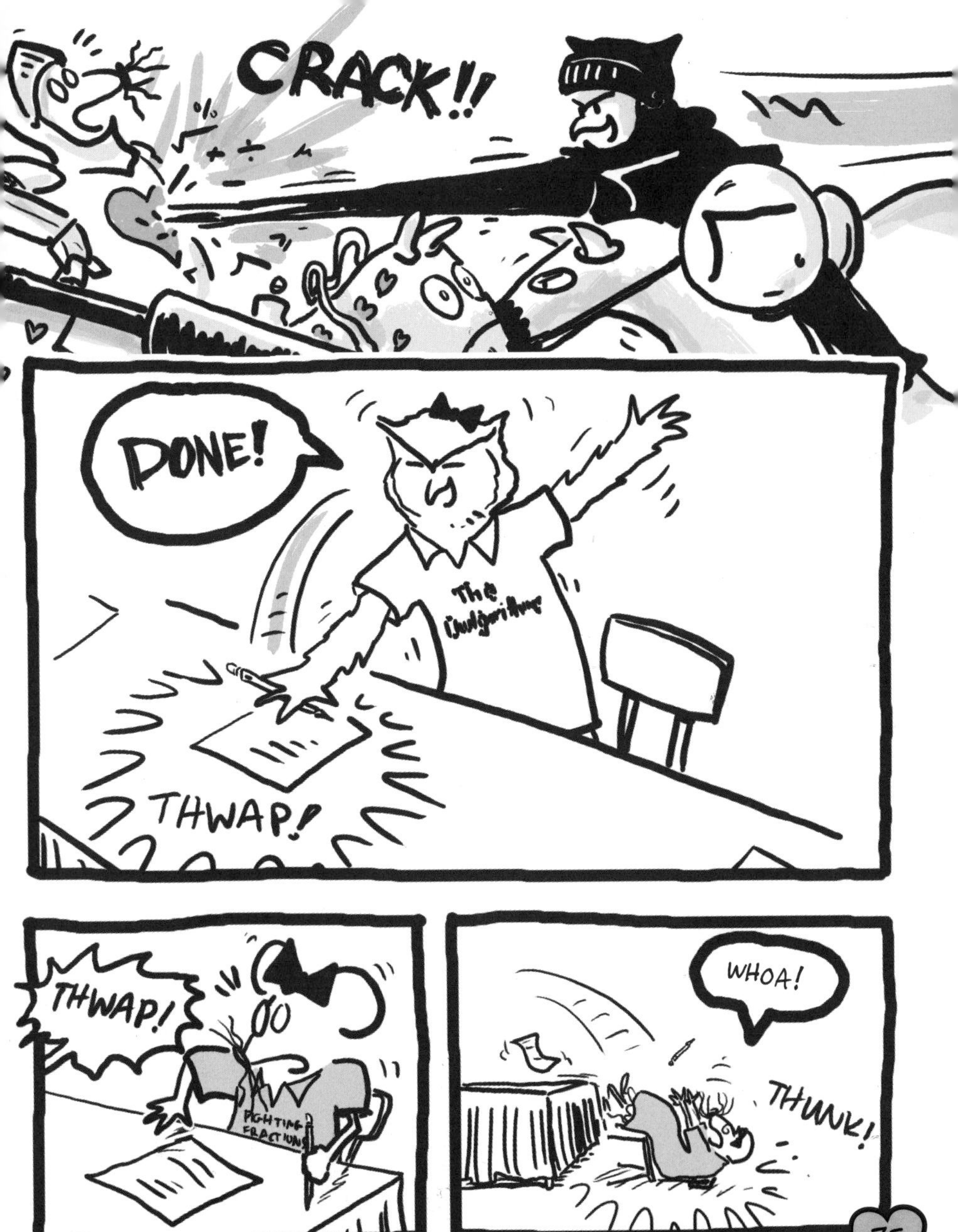
CRACK!!
DONE!
The Owlgorithms
THWAP!
THWAP!
FIGHTING FRACTIONS
WHOA!
THUNK!

HOOT HOOT! THAT WAS A CLASSIC! HOOT!
HOOT! HOOT! WHAT DO YOU EXPECT FROM
FILTHY, DIRTY, DISEASE-CARRYING RODE
HOOT HOOT HOOT! ALL THEY'RE GOOD FOR
SNACKS! HOOT! HOOT! HOOT! HA! WHAT'VE
I'VE NEVER ... PATHETIC
HOOT HO... EN GET
INTO TH... T! HO
DO THEY ... RY FOR

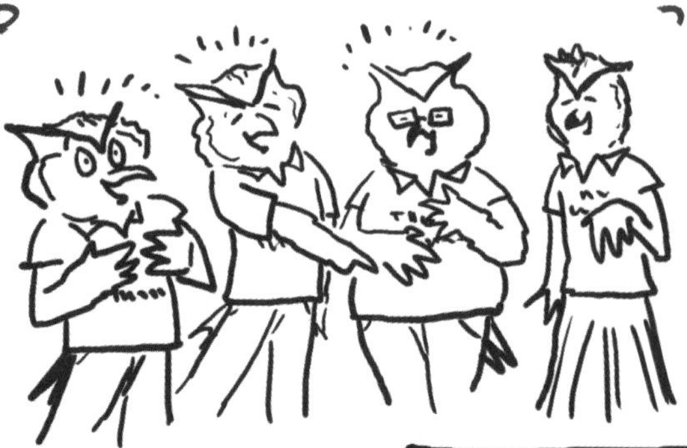

KINDERGARTNERS? HO
GET A BODY BAG! HOOT
WAS THE QUICKEST LOS
THE WORLD! HOOT! HOO
A... THIS TALK ABOUT

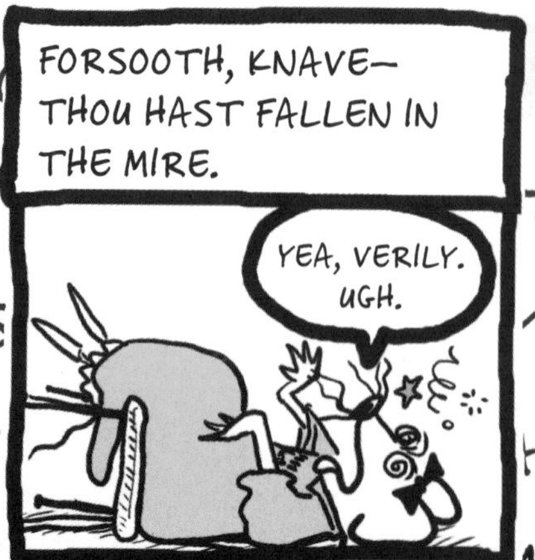
FORSOOTH, KNAVE—
THOU HAST FALLEN IN
THE MIRE.
YEA, VERILY.
UGH.

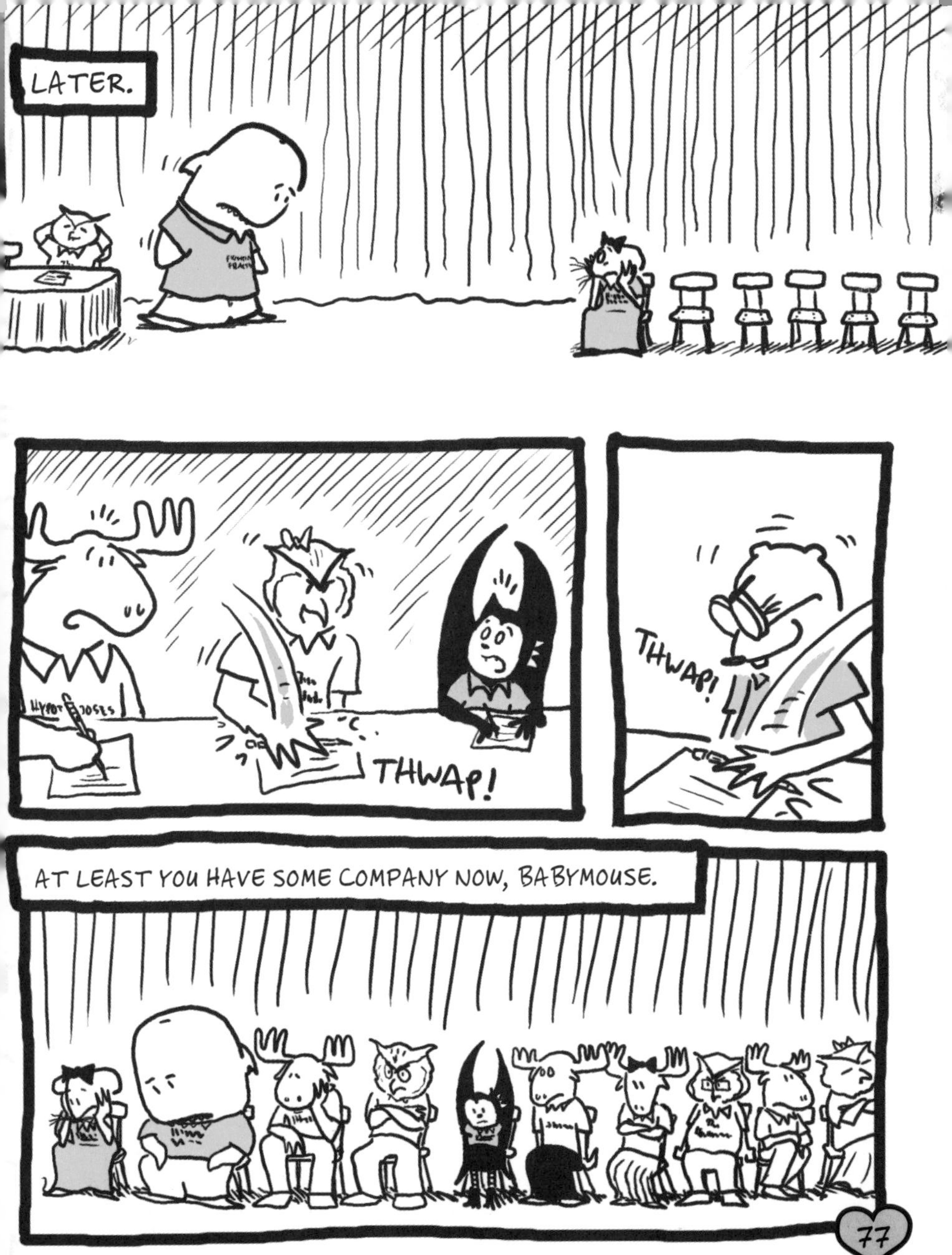
LATER.
THWAP!
THWAP!
AT LEAST YOU HAVE SOME COMPANY NOW, BABYMOUSE.

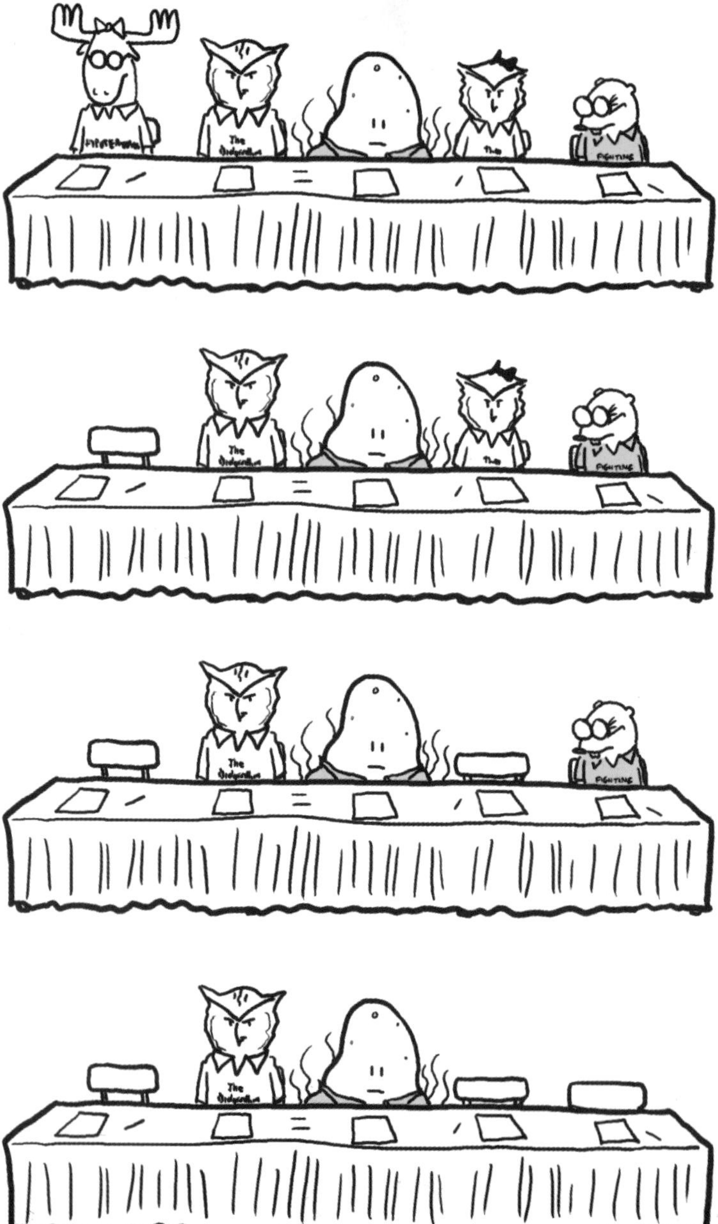
The
The
FIGHTING

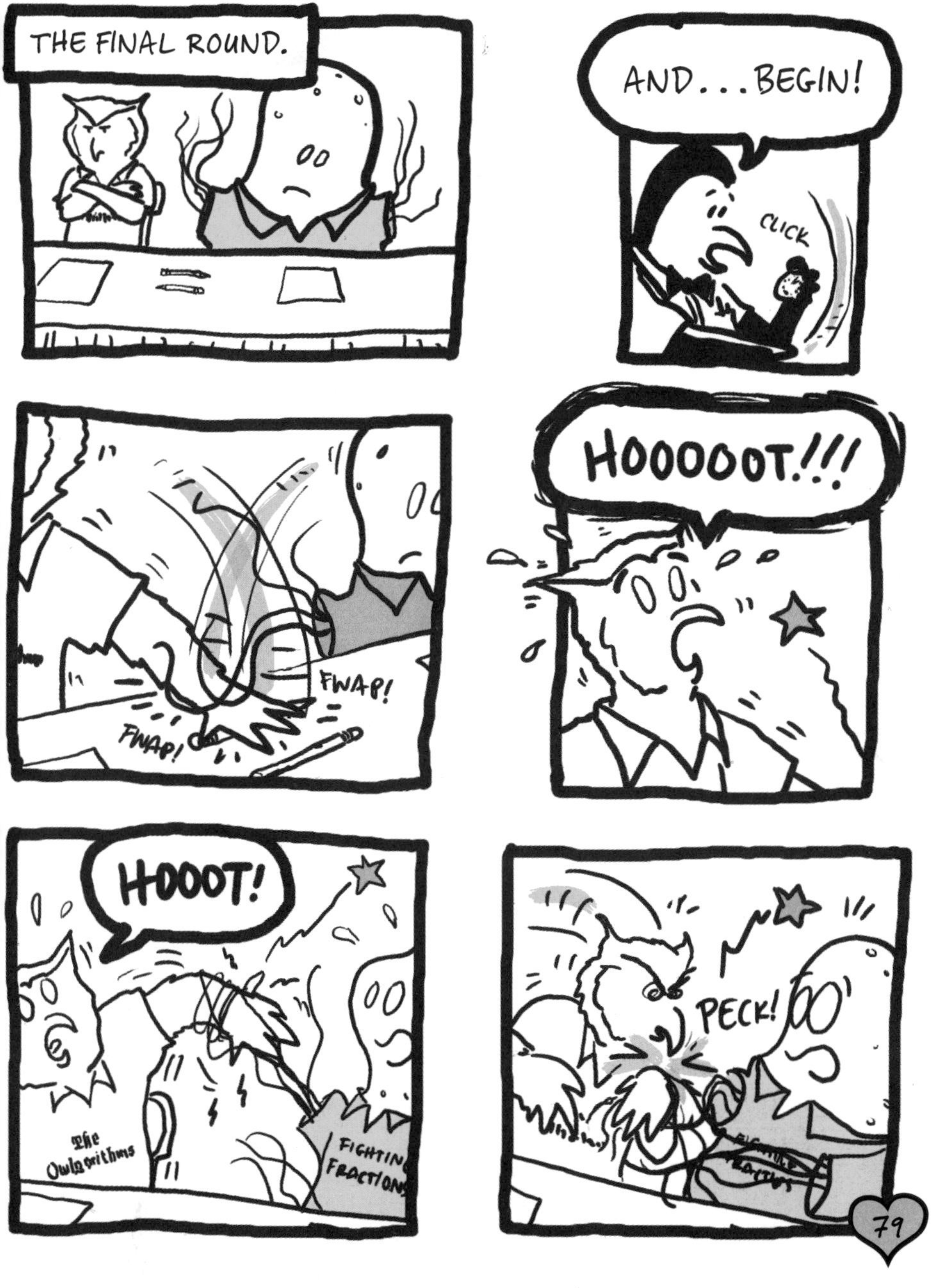
THE FINAL ROUND.
AND . . . BEGIN!
CLICK
FWAP!
FWAP!
HOOOOOT!!!
HOOOT!
The Owlgorithms
FIGHTING FRACTIONS
PECK!

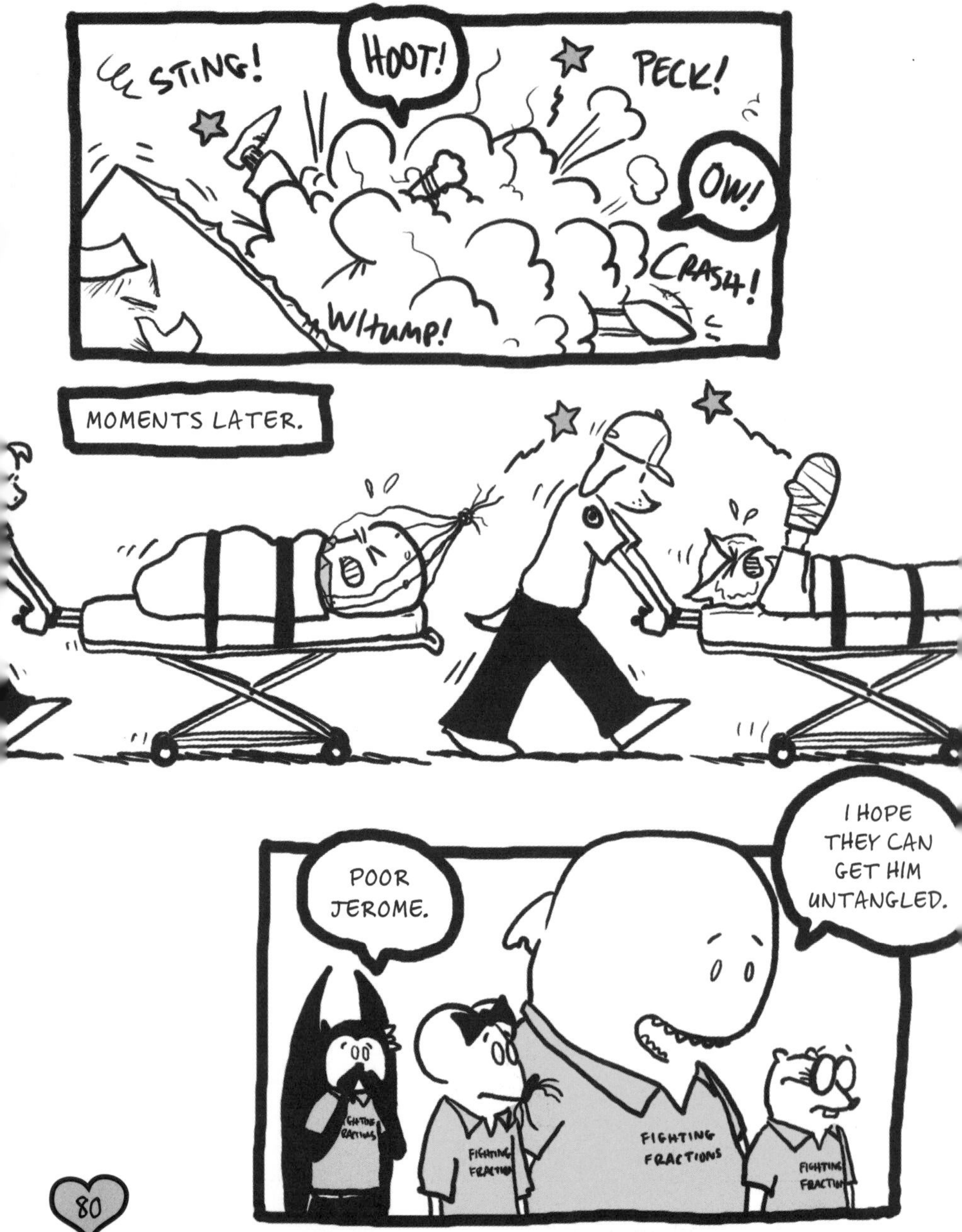
STING!
HOOT!
PECK!
OW!
CRASH!
WHUMP!
MOMENTS LATER.
POOR JEROME.
I HOPE THEY CAN GET HIM UNTANGLED.
FIGHTING FRACTIONS

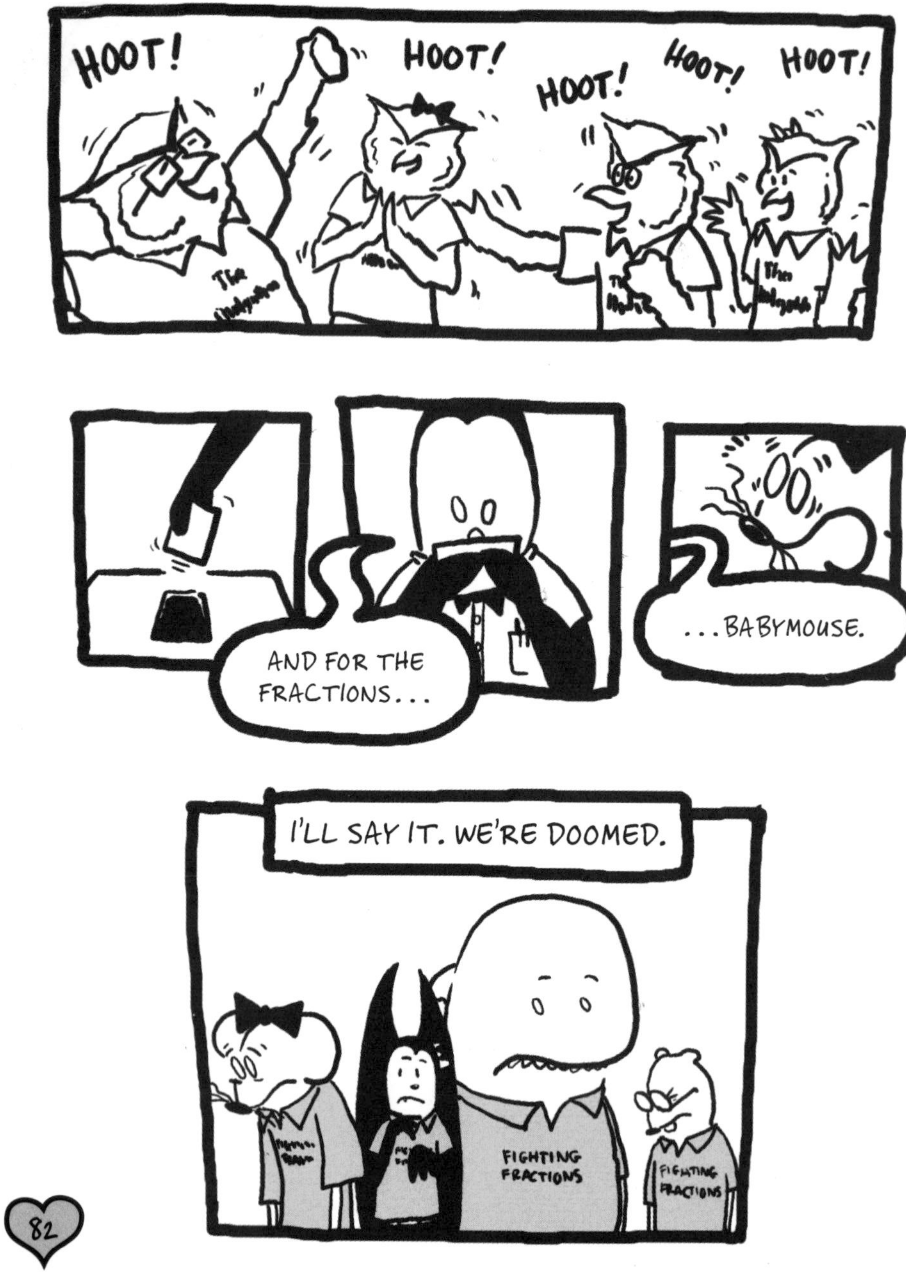
HOOT!
HOOT!
HOOT!
HOOT!
HOOT!
AND FOR THE FRACTIONS...
...BABYMOUSE.
I'LL SAY IT. WE'RE DOOMED.
FIGHTING FRACTIONS
FIGHTING FRACTIONS

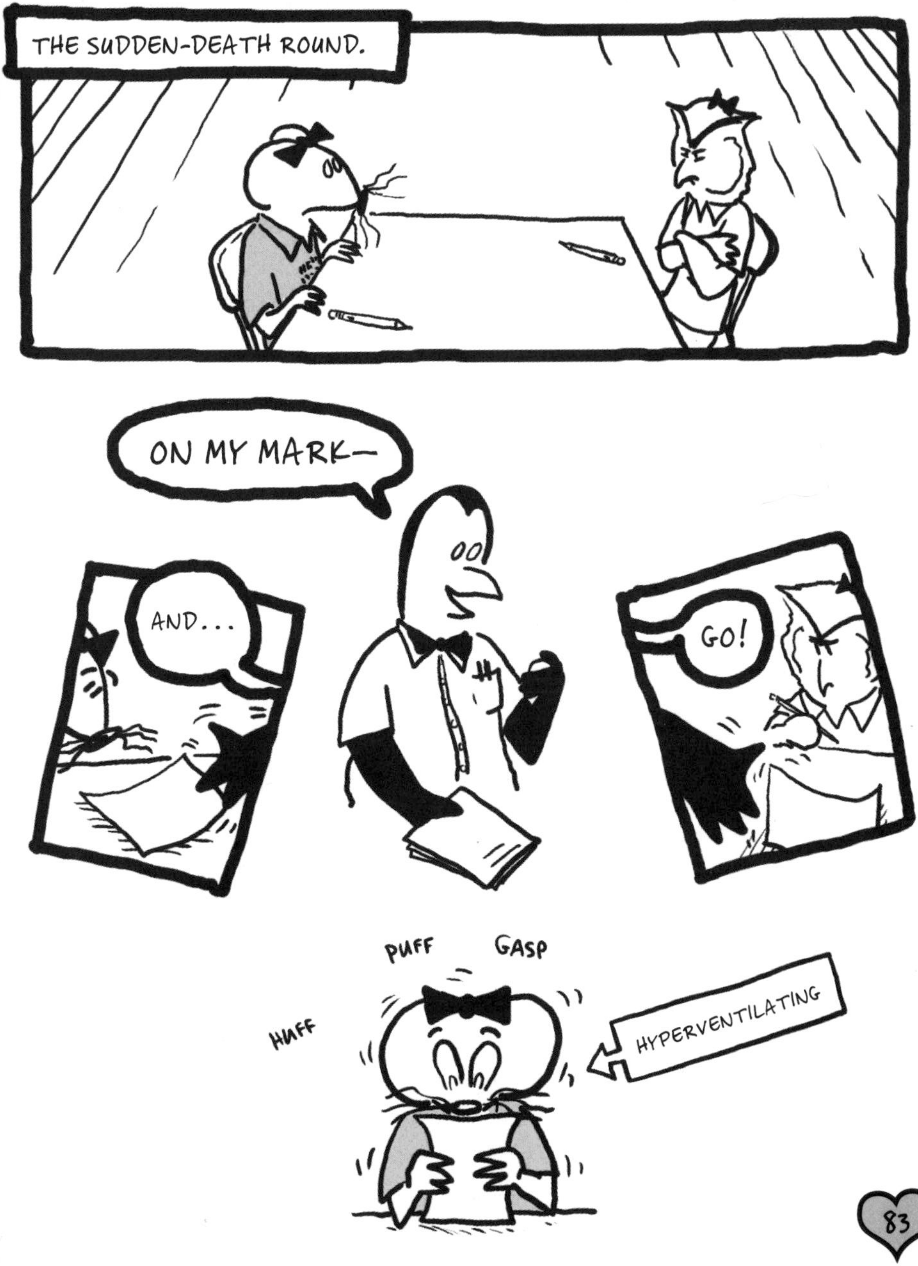
THE SUDDEN-DEATH ROUND.
ON MY MARK—
AND...
GO!
PUFF
GASP
HUFF
HYPERVENTILATING

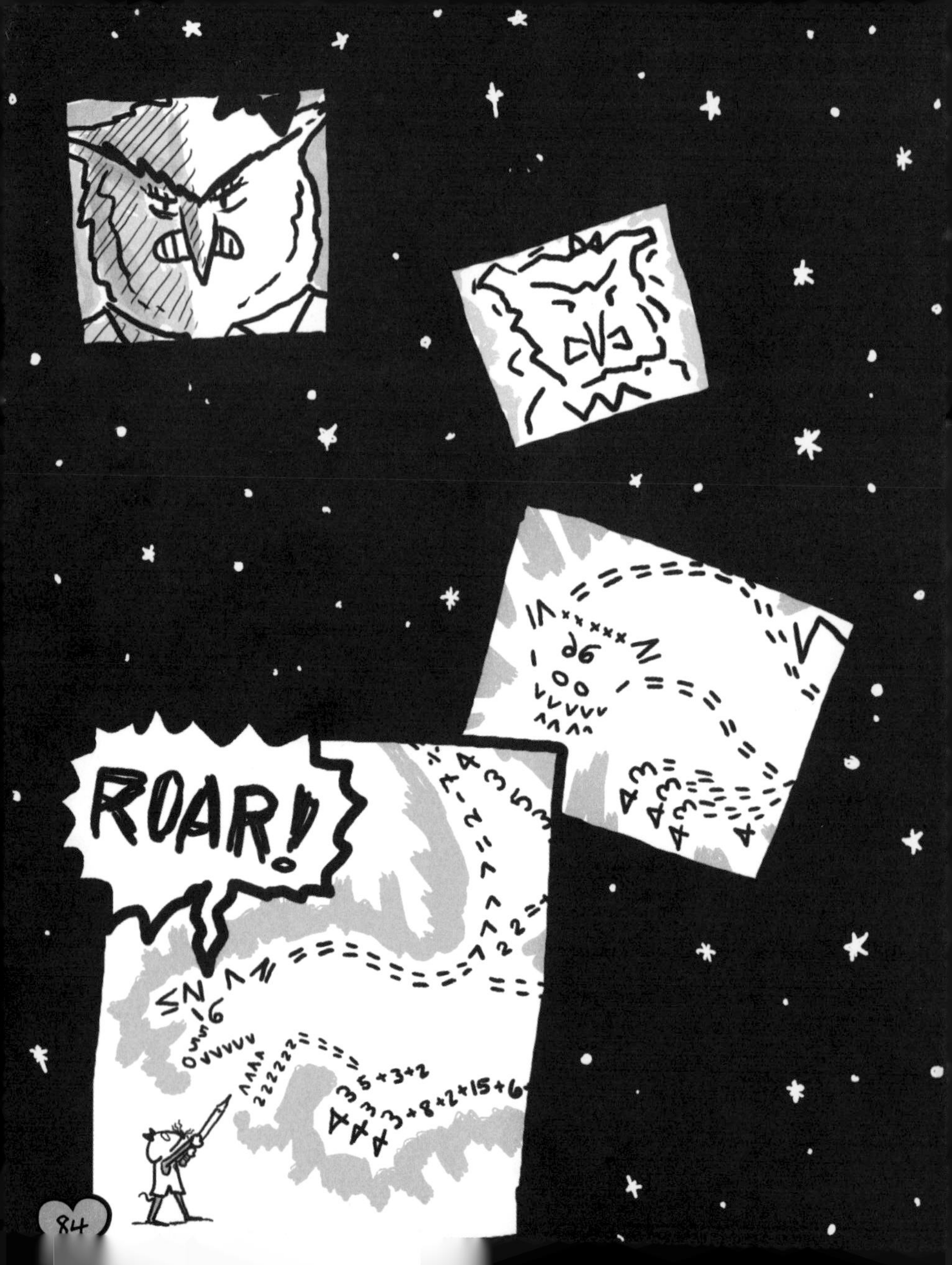
ROAR!

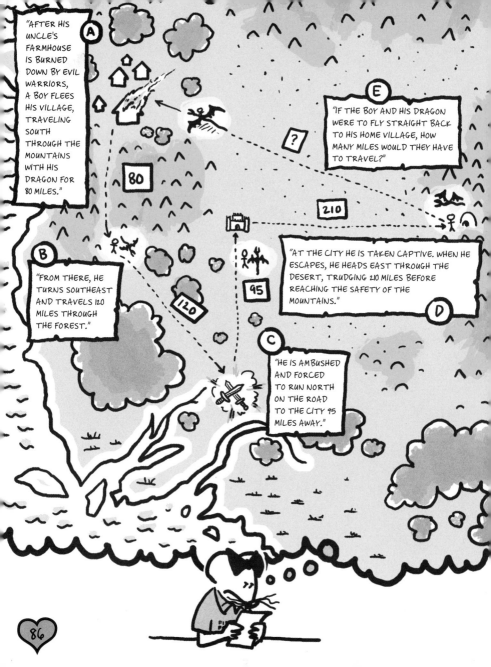

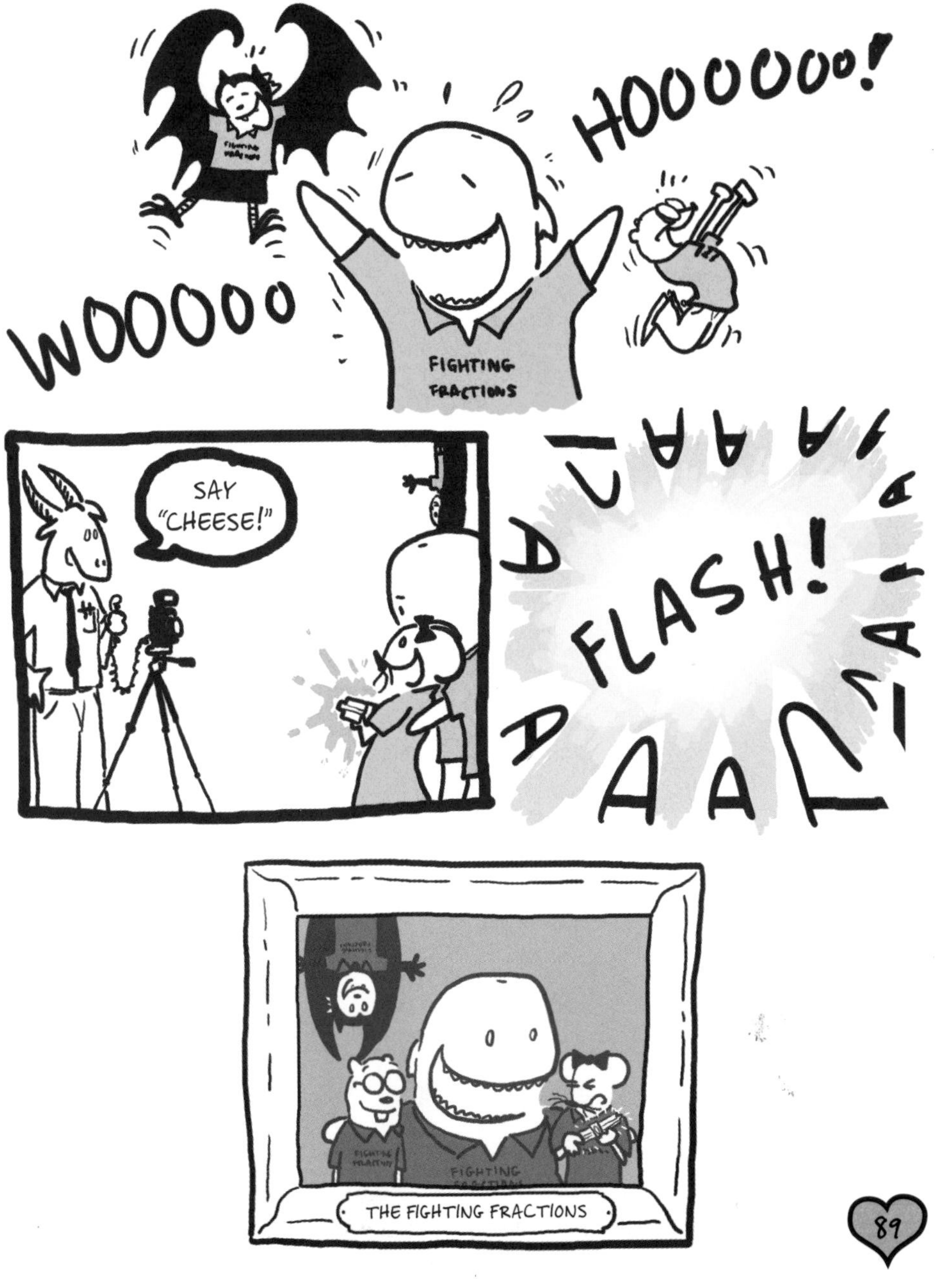

WOOOOO
HOOOOOO!
FIGHTING FRACTIONS
SAY "CHEESE!"
AAAAAA
FLASH!
THE FIGHTING FRACTIONS

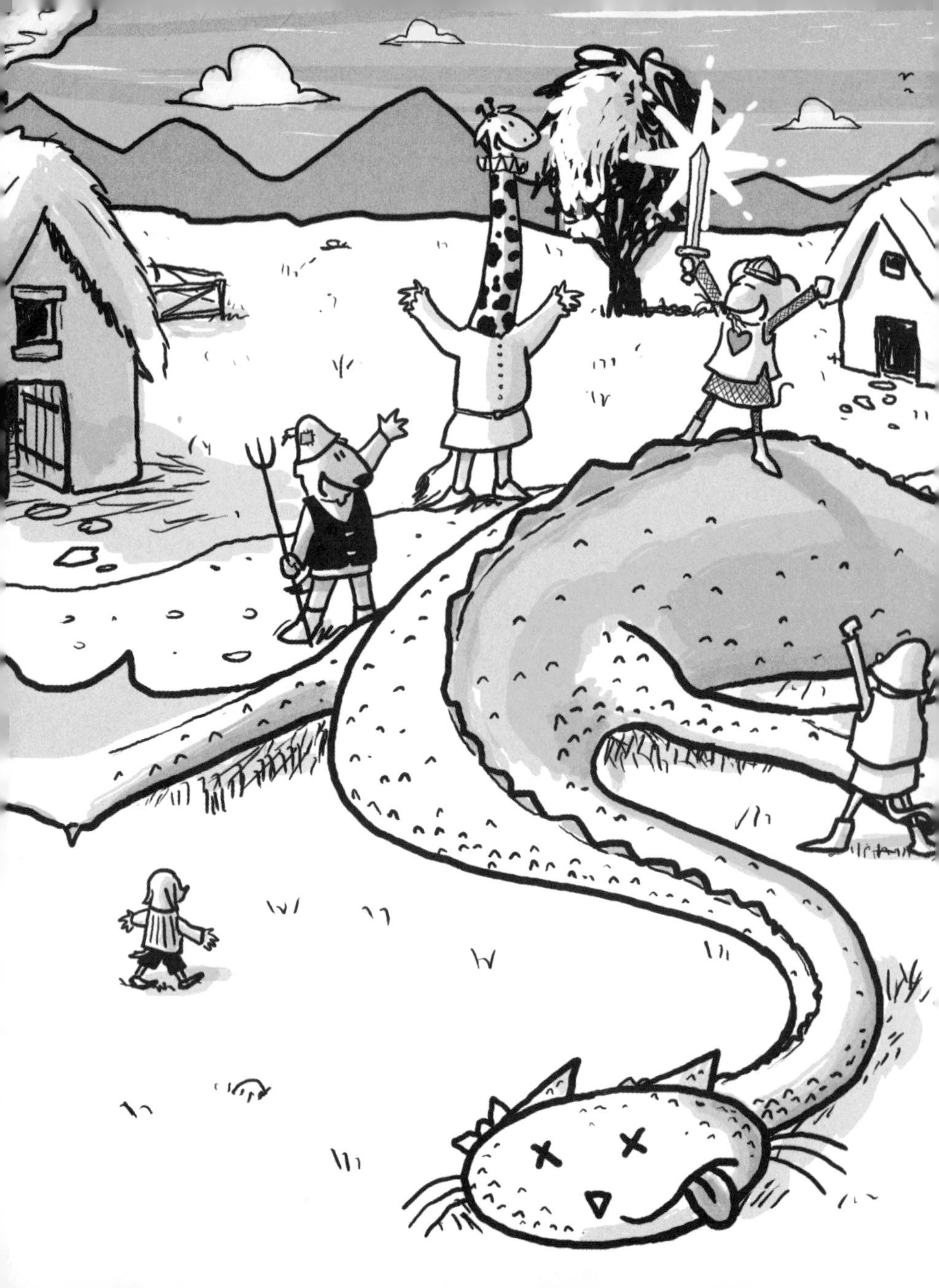

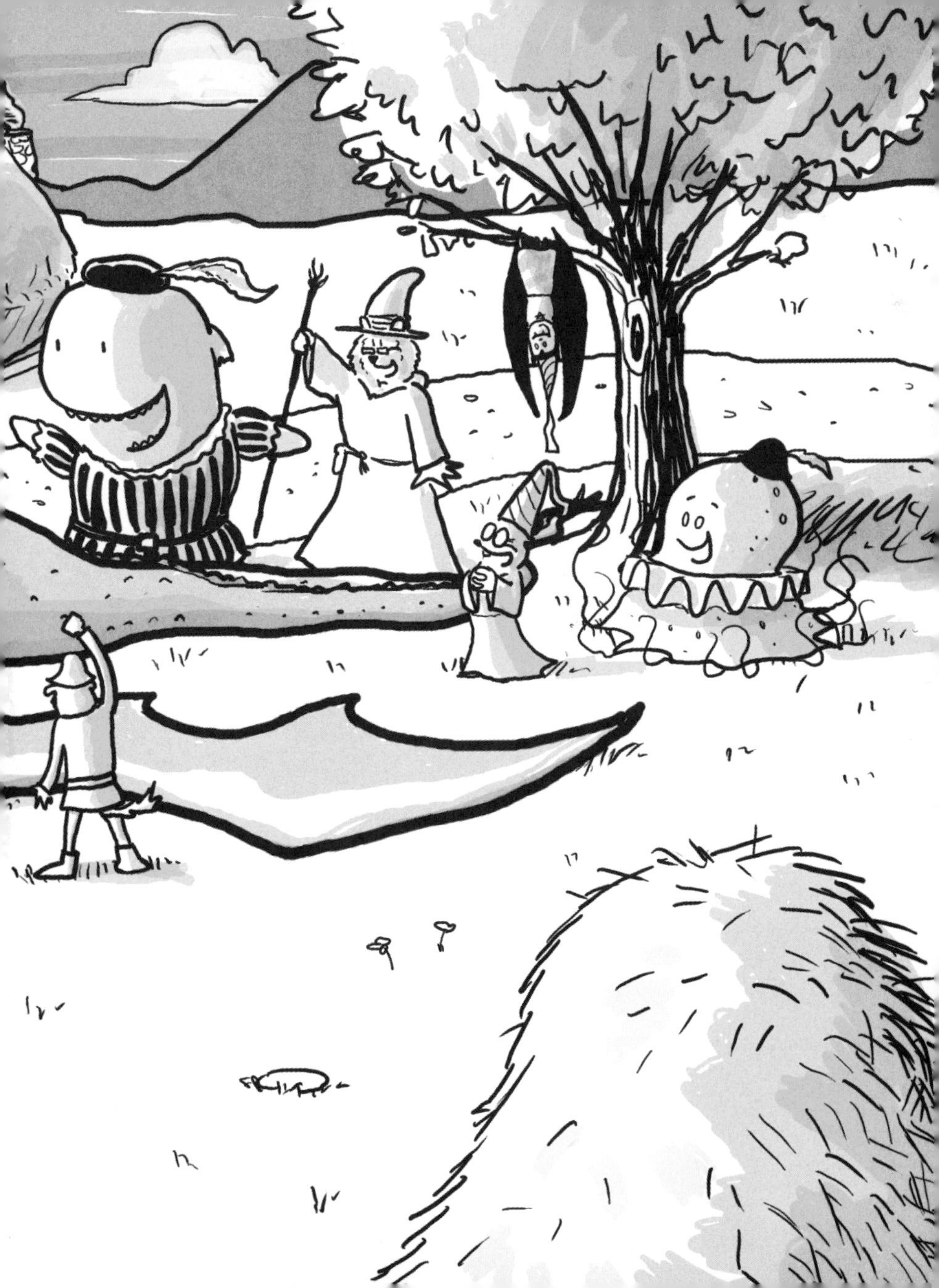

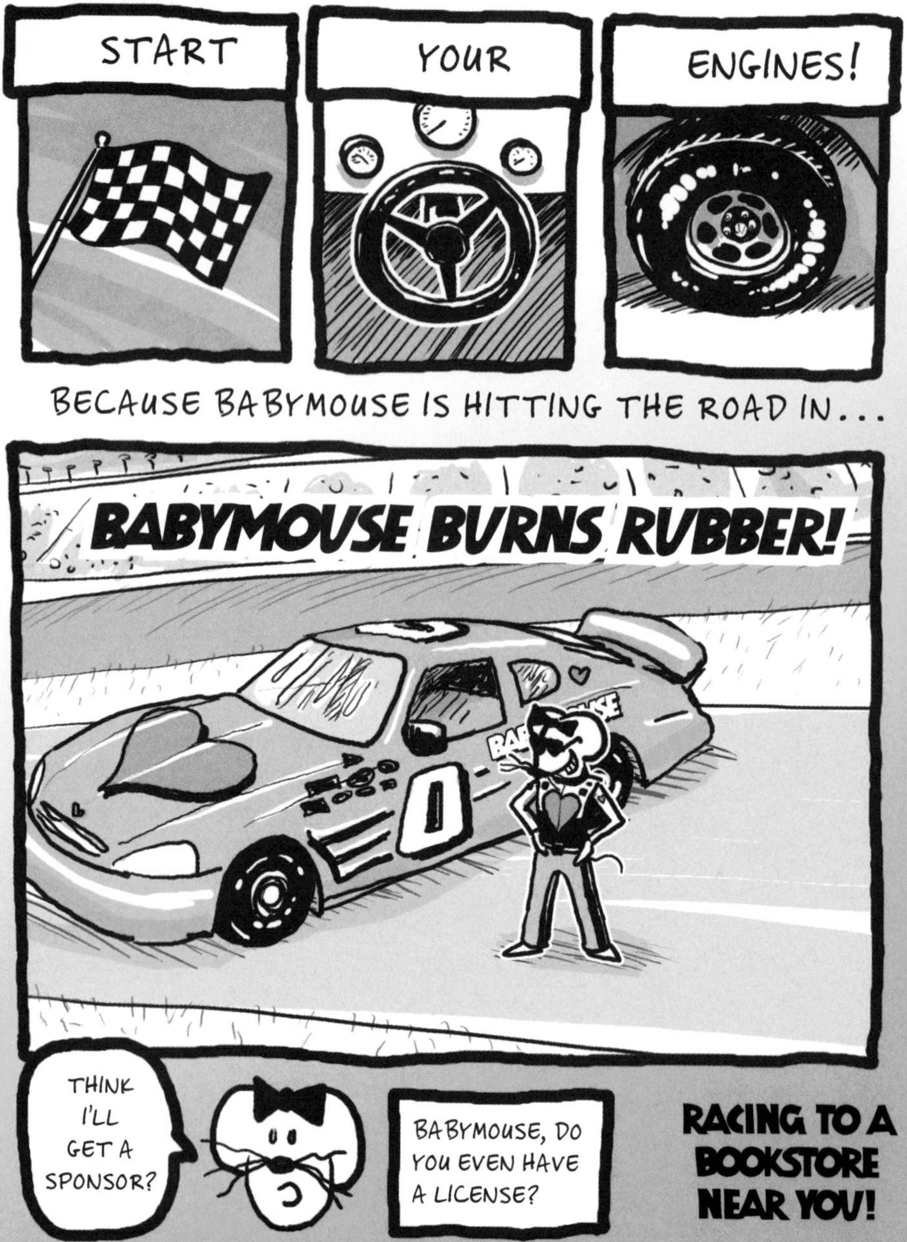
START
YOUR
ENGINES!
BECAUSE BABYMOUSE IS HITTING THE ROAD IN...
BABYMOUSE BURNS RUBBER!
THINK I'LL GET A SPONSOR?
BABYMOUSE, DO YOU EVEN HAVE A LICENSE?
RACING TO A BOOKSTORE NEAR YOU!

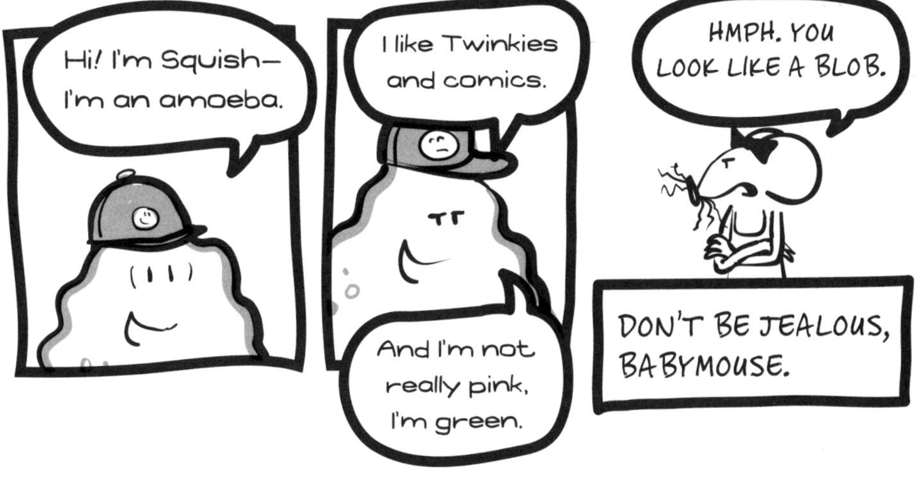
Hi! I'm Squish—
I'm an amoeba.
I like Twinkies
and comics.
And I'm not
really pink,
I'm green.
HMPH. YOU
LOOK LIKE A BLOB.
DON'T BE JEALOUS,
BABYMOUSE.

READ ABOUT SQUISH'S AMAZING ADVENTURES IN:

#1 SQUISH: Super Amoeba

#2 SQUISH: Brave New Pond

#3 SQUISH: The Power of the Parasite

#4 SQUISH: Captain Disaster

#5 SQUISH: Game On!

AND COMING SOON:

#6 SQUISH: Fear the Amoeba

★ "IF EVER A NEW SERIES DESERVED TO GO VIRAL, THIS ONE DOES."
—*KIRKUS REVIEWS*, STARRED

If you like Babymouse,
you'll love these other great books
by Jennifer L. Holm!

THE BOSTON JANE TRILOGY
EIGHTH GRADE IS MAKING ME SICK
MIDDLE SCHOOL IS WORSE THAN MEATLOAF
OUR ONLY MAY AMELIA
PENNY FROM HEAVEN
TURTLE IN PARADISE

THEY'RE
REALLY GOOD!
TRUST ME!